THE COMING OF STEELEYE

The single guard levelled a Zonal Catheter at
Steeleye's body. Had the guard been given the
opportunity to use the weapon Steeleye's body
would have drained of its life blood in seconds
leaving only a heap of flesh, but his mind was
too sharp, his senses too alert. He caught the
tense grip of the guard's mind as he prepared
to attack with the Catheter. The Sylvan hid his
body behind a support at the back of the auditorium.
The deadly eye might not have found its aim
quickly enough, and Steeleye's body was vulnerable
in the centre of the stage. With speed bewildering
to those still watching, he swept across the rows
of tables and chairs, darting in and out, weaving
back and forth, making the guard's aim impossible.
As he went he displayed a little of his own
magic. Employing the body-motion skills inherent
in his structure he altered size, shape and
meaning, taking a low, smooth form which
slithered like a snake through the escaping
Sylvan audience.

Reaching the space where the guard still stood,
watching for his quarry, Steeleye drew up to his
full height, and without warning sent a single
streak of fire from his head and levelled the
Sylvan guard to the ground. In a three step
movement he turne⬚⬚⬚⬚⬚⬚⬚⬚⬚⬚⬚⬚⬚⬚
groups of guards, t⬚⬚⬚⬚⬚⬚⬚⬚⬚⬚⬚⬚⬚
in his huge hand, d⬚⬚⬚⬚⬚⬚⬚⬚⬚⬚⬚
against the wall.

Then he reached and hooked out two blankets, turned again he lifted exactly and, gently laid him his helpless body

The Coming of Steeleye

The first book in the Steeleye saga

Saul Dunn

CORONET BOOKS
Hodder and Stoughton

Printed and bound in Great Britain
for Coronet Books,
Hodder and Stoughton
London.
By C. Nicholls & Company Ltd.
The Philips Park Press, Manchester

ISBN 0 340 20507 5

PART I

The Lull

In the latter years of the Sylvan Empire a Man was born, full grown on Zrost then detached from the Federation. His full name was Havoc Carls and he remains till today the greatest single influence in the civilised Universe.

When the Sylvans believed themselves omnipotent this Man emerged in the likeness of a dead race to destroy their rule, and became known as Steeleye. His escapades, his deeds of bravery, his rule of many lands, his strength, intellect, craft and criminal acts mark him as the most significant living creature ever to walk the planets of Freefall, for there has been no other such as Steeleye, and in his wake there can be none to equal him.

The opening lines of Haephranis' *Biographies of Steeleye*, Universal Annals ref. hfgt/546.

Chapter 1

Tarash leaned painfully down, tending the force-topped
Vegitators. One thousand and fifty, one thousand and
fifty-one, one thousand and fifty-two, one thousand and
. . . he lifted his mis-shapen head and peered uselessly,
forlornly across the long low structures before him.
Thousands more, many thousands, stretching before him
for ever, all containing the same carefully cultured
edibles. All for the mouths of the Sylvans on their
mighty planets in the Complex.

Tarash's face mirrored nothing but exhaustion. One
hand operated the fertility tester, the other tended his
aching back. The land was open, the cold cruel, the
isolation total.

One thousand and sixty-two, one thousand and sixty-
three, one thousand and . . . a sound.

One thousand and sixty-five, one thousand and sixty . . .
the same sound . . . a step.

One thousand and sixty-seven, one . . . again, a step, a
scratch of foot against thin ground. What?

One thousand and sixty-nine . . . Tarash raised his head,
weary but frowning, his body motioning slightly,
twisting, the molecules displaced through nervous
tension, through fear. He stood up, as straight as his
frame would allow, and searched the area around him,
unable to see far into the grey darkness, narrowing
his feeble eyes against the wall of no light. The mists of
Cathandramis were falling now, the great haars from the
mountains around. He would soon finish work, soon
return to his empty, lonely home and sleep. And when
he had slept he would rise and start work again, and so

7

it would be tomorrow, and tomorrow, and for ever, until he died on the spot that he worked.

He could see nothing, but still he looked, warned by his old instincts, feeling the atmosphere of danger.

But there was nothing.

One thousand and seventy, one thousand and seventy-one . . .

"Tarash."

The wind stopped, the world stopped, life almost stopped for Tarash. He dropped the tester, pulled his back straight, body-motioned furiously, his long accustomed molecular changes twisting his whole shape out of proportion. His slow mind raced. Before him moving without movement out of the mist, was a figure. A vast giant of a creature, measuring surely four metres. Broad, strong-armed, great powerful legs swollen with muscle, iron-fibred, rooted to the swirling misty ground.

"Tarash."

Death was upon him. The figure moved without motion, no body-changing, no nervous demeanour, no fear, absolute power. Like a robot on an air base the figure continued to advance upon poor Tarash; with arms folded on the heavy chest it stared. The body was covered in a skincloth, red and black, belted about fibrous muscular flesh, alive without doubt, burning with vibrating dominance. The head was huge, noble, with an aquiline nose, full red lips and an eye, one terrible steel eye alongside a normal living eye. The single eye flourished with silvered threats, sparkled as it caught the artificial lights around the enclosure, flashed horror.

Tarash wavered almost to the point of liquid, his body broken with the sight of this monster, moving in on him, coming to kill him surely, to end his life for ever.

"Fear not Tarash, I come not to kill you, but to borrow you."

"Who are . . .?"

"That is not your concern Tarash, you will live again. I have only need of you for a while; do not fear."

Tarash picked up the tester and flung it with all the remaining strength in his body, hurling it wildly at the intruder.

The steel eye glowed red, burnished from silvery steel to a dreadful burning red, the heat catching the tester and reducing it to nothing. Tarash fell back under the blast and grasped for the covered Vegitators, desperately trying to get away, hopelessly clinging to life. He ran for all he was worth, dashing everything before him, smashing the solar plates under his feet. But he got only a few metres, then he turned and the great creature was behind him, arms outstretched, lifting him bodily from the ground, rising into the air. Tarash lost consciousness.

Chapter 2

No one bothered you in the Federation unless you bothered them. The Federation of Universal Powers allowed anyone to travel between planets any time. No fuss, just get on with your business and life will be sweet.

Tourism was not so much an industry as a way of life, particularly around the Central Administrative Complex. Out of the forty million planets inhabited in the Empire, the most popular was the Sylvan Complex, right slap in the middle of the Sylvan Empire, or the Federation, or the FUP, call it what you will.

You could go by "Travelaunch", you could "Sail the Skies in a Sylvan Galleon" – and it really looked like a galleon, but it moved at the speed of light. Or if the distances were really great, you could teleport.

Tarash would have gone the slowest way. The real Tarash, that is. From Cathandramis to the complex would have taken four months. But it was safe. Tarash, however, was not there. The real Tarash, that is. The Man that was now Tarash chose to teleport, the most dangerous method of travel in space but the fastest. One quarter of a light year in three seconds, the time it takes to disrupt and reinstate a living body.

The best known ad-line for the "Travelaunch" was accurate enough: "If you were told by a teleport guide that there was a twelve per cent chance that you would never reach your destination, would you go? Travel Travelaunch, it's safe."

But this Tarash was in a hurry, he was always in a hurry. He approached the Security desk in the shuffling manner of the old farmer he was duplicating, one foot slightly deformed. He bowed his mis-shapen head the way Tarash had bowed his as he had shifted across the vast cultivated land of Cathandramis, the agricultural world, feeding the Sylvans in their nine-planet complex.

Tarash had been an obvious choice. His average build and appearance suited our Man's needs perfectly. Taking on the Sylvan's appearance was no problem, and poor Tarash would suffer no great hardship being confined to a force beam for a few weeks.

"Teleporters to Sylvan Six go to gate 987 now."

That was him. He shuffled. Cathandramis to Sylvan Six, the entry point to the Sylvan Complex from this planet.

"ID?"

The well-preserved and little-used disc passed hands.

"Name?"

"Tarash."

"Employment?"

"Agricultural technician."

"Purpose?"

"Eh?"

"Purpose, purpose of visit." The guard scowled. Extra words were an irritation.

"Holiday."

"Hmph, some holiday you'll get on Anchor."

No answer.

"I suppose you *are* going to Anchor?"

"Yes."

"That's where they all go from here. Sylvan Six then Anchor. You're wasting your time buddy, there's nothing to see."

Silence.

"OK, get in the chamber."

Almost like a death sentence, but too late now. He had passed the checks, one by the guard and one unseen. The guard had been easy, the rest was silent: body wave tests, brain tests, ID confirmation, prints – everything had to be perfect. For the seconds when Tarash, or the Man who was now Tarash, went through that screening he had to duplicate *the* Tarash exactly. Not an easy task for anyone, let alone a Man. But he had evidently passed. All was done without sound, not a mutter or a squeak. But if you were not accepted, then you heard about it. Nevertheless, the "arrest chutes" were quick and silent. The only noise you heard was your own voice as you disappeared, maybe for ever. Just a scream, cut off as the chutes shut . . . tight.

The new Tarash was just ready to take his place in the teleport chamber when he heard a scuffle a few feet away, to his right. He turned to see a creature which did not resemble any in the immediate flight area, fighting for his life.

The creature was a Farmish, carrying enormous weight made up of fat and muscle on a huge body, almost three times the overall size of the average Sylvan. He suffered the disadvantage of a slightly stronger gravitational pressure on Sylvan Six than he was accustomed to, but this did not seem unduly to hamper his progress through the crowd of guards now gathered about him. He cast them into the air like an auto-harvester cutting through corn, thrashing like a giant rotary arm, cursing all the while.

It was not at all clear what he had done, but the ensuing chaos gave Tarash a clear way through to the teleport chamber, through the final check-point guards who were intent on aiding their battered comrades.

The Farmish turned his great head and spotted a guard levelling his weapon; he reached out a huge arm and swept the helpless Sylvan off his feet and into the arms of five others who had hoped to stop the monster.

He had some direct purpose in mind and Tarash stopped to watch for a moment as he picked up two guards and held them before him. His great voice bellowed out.

"I will kill these two guards and many others with my

12

bare hands if you do not send for Trok. Bring Trok to me, I would speak with him now." The echoing deep voice crashed across the flight area and a guard spoke into a video telephone.

"I will speak with Trok, where is he?"

"He comes directly, he will be here in moments, do not harm the guards."

The Farmish remained holding the guards up with apparent ease and waited without further word or movement until there was a scuffle on the entrance platform and a group of very official guards entered, led by one who wore the insignia of Security leadership. This must be Trok himself. He was square, absolutely solid, every inch of his sturdy body strung together by rock-hard steel muscles from many years of physical exertion and combat. It was rumoured that he fought each day with five Sylvan Security guards specially selected for their size and strength. They were dressed in leather and metal armour to protect them from Trock's blows, which he never pulled. He killed his opponents frequently, simply by accident, their heads smashed by the horrific blows of their leader. His black, greased hair was tightly forced against his head and the square set of his face seemed almost to have muscles of its own that might leap out and hit you. His neck was short – sometimes it seemed as if he had no neck at all – and he was not renowned for his body-motion abilities. Some said that he was not a Sylvan at all. He did not resemble one and he kept his body straight, without the strange and characteristic meanderings of most Sylvans.

As leader of the Sylvan Security forces he was so far indomitable, feared by everyone, though apparently not by the Farmish.

"Here comes the great Trok." The enormous creature lifted the two guards in the air and deliberately, with a show of strength, smashed their skulls against each other, casting the limp bodies to one side as he strode towards Trok, who stood his ground as though he had grown there.

"You . . . I have longed to meet you thus Trok, for years I have longed to meet you thus." With the strange medieval tongue common only to the Farmish, the great monster stepped closer.

"Whatever you have to say to me Farmish, say it and be done, I have no time for dramatic gestures." Trok spoke calmly but with an edge to his voice like a battle cry. Every word he spoke told all those who would cross him to think again.

"I am here to kill you and take back your head to Farmish Planet, where I will stick it on a stake and put the stake on the grave of my family, whom you slaughtered in cold blood, Trok. You killed them along with hundreds of others."

"The Farmish were going against the law, I simply taught them a lesson. If your family were amongst those who died, then it was unfortunate that you were not with them." Trok spat at the feet of the giant before him.

The Farmish was at least twice Trok's height, towering over him, grimacing with anger and pain down at the midget of a Sylvan. But the fight that ensued was unequal the other way. Trok's skills as a warrior, even in hand-to-hand battle, were manifest. The Farmish lunged at the Security leader, thrashing with a huge blow aimed at Trok's head which missed. Trok grasped the great thick wrist and pulled, using the giant's momentum to carry him past. As he went Trok deposited a series of five or six sharp blows to the Farmish's neck.

As if bitten by an unpleasant fly the Farmish grasped his neck and turned to Trok again.

"You can try to kill me, Farmish, but I will show you no mercy when you lose."

"And I will show thee death, Trok."

The great four-metre giant grasped Trok unexpectedly about the body, each hand on each shoulder, and lifted him off the ground; but before any damage could be done Trok swung his whole powerful body forward and kicked his opponent in the face with both heels, drawing blood from the nose and mouth. Trok got up from his fallen position and without a moment's hesitation delivered a dreadful blow, with both fists wrapped together, to the side of the Farmish's head, catching him on the temple. Not satisfied with this he leapt into the air and thrust a muscular leg out, delivering what would have been a fatal blow to any Sylvan, square to the throat, powerful enough to thrust the vocal chamber into the spinal cord. But although the Farmish choked and spat up blood he did not die, or even drop to his knees. Instead, he grasped for Trok again, missing his body but catching and twisting his arm, evidently painfully. Trok stepped back, shocked by the mammoth strength of the Farmish, and decided to waste no more time on showing off his fighting technique. He drew a four-bladed knife from his belt and hurled it at the Farmish's head. The Farmish lifted his hand at the right moment and lost it, severed clean from his wrist. He had lost a hand but saved his life, for a moment at least. He clutched the bleeding stump and, incensed by pain, began to blunder about the area, trampling everything and everyone under foot. He must have killed at least a dozen Sylvan bystanders as he waived his bloody arm at Trok. It could not last long, and as Tarash watched, a guard drew his blaster and dispatched the wild Farmish with a shot to the chest. The monster reeled once more with a cavernous smoking hole in his great chest and crashed to the ground, amidst scampering Sylvans.

A dramatic scene, and proof of only one of the awful deeds to which Trok could be named culpable.

The Farmish's body was pushed towards an arrest shute and it disappeared down into the depths of the unknown, Sylvans peering after it. Tarash turned to the teleport chamber and stepped in. The Tarash who was not Tarash, . . . was no ordinary farm labourer from a planet in the Sylvan Universe. This was no shuffling, bowed peasant worker, sweating away his life to serve his Sylvan masters. This was Steeleye. *The* Steeleye, and he did nothing by half measures. Tarash had been duplicated for the seconds necessary to take him through the tests, exactly, perfectly, without blemish, without a mark unattributable to the beaten old body or a thought bent from the dim-witted mind. The chamber doors shut with a smooth swish, and the guard threw the disrupter into "go." Quietly, though, Steeleye thanked the dead Farmish for his inadvertent help.

"Please stand still. Do not be disturbed by any sounds or feelings you may experience. When the light is red before you, you have arrived at your destination."

Steeleye flinched. An almost imperceptible flinch as he braced himself for the transporter's strange delivery of his body and mind, hopefully still intact, onto Sylva. But it was enough. The Circle saw. The Circle noted.

And then the red light shone and Steeleye was one of the eighty-eight per cent success stories — a credit to the teleport agencies, and alive.

The planetary Complex of Sylva was made up of nine interconnected worlds. Once upon a time there had been only one: Anchor, the central planet. With a rapidly expanding Empire the Sylvans, ever certain of centralisation, transported other planetary bodies and attached them by transtubes to the central body, encircling all nine planets with a force barrier quite impenetrable from without. Approaching by Travelaunch it was a vast, mirrored sphere. You could not see through, you could see only your reflection; but once entered, the skies were star-speckled outside.

Each planet was connected to all others by transtubes and by thin, almost invisible, moving force fields. Again it could be fun for the tourist. You could take the transtubes, swish up or down a "light lift" and be there in seconds, or you could slide along a "force thread," riding down a stream of light, and arrive unharmed on the planet of your choice. Incongruously poetic for such unromantic people.

Anchor was the central point of administration and housed the Sylvan Palaces where the High Councillors ruled. These Councillors were known as the Sylvas, and their power was and always had been absolute. The other eight planets surrounding the centre were numbered: Sylva One to Eight. Each planet coped with a designated portion of the vast task of controlling and overseeing a colossal Empire, stretching almost endlessly across space. Forty million inhabited planets, countless lives, countless breeds, massive power.

Steeleye, as Tarash, stepped from the teleport chamber and crossed the short ground to the exit barriers.

"Cabs to all levels."

"Choose your accommodation: hotels, motels, apartments for privacy; Sylva Six is yours. We are here to serve your pleasure," the signs read.

"Fix your credit. Any place referenced. Make your stay good to remember, carry a TI Recorder. Replay your seconds back home. Give the family your trip on a 4D same time transmitter." A TI transmitter was a portable Telepathic Insinuator which, should you require such invasion of your privacy, would pick up all your thoughts and activities and relay them through a 4D recorder to your home.

Steeleye shuffled to the main Travel Centre Exit and hailed a ground cab. Time was precious. Any false move could give him away, and time meant chances. But he had to get familiarised. He had to take as much of this strange place away with him as he could in his mind, for later.

The ground cab slid forward.

"Place?"

"Centre."

The driver body-motioned and Steeleye sat back in the

smooth rest. Across ground he got his first real view of a Sylvan planet. It was all devoted to either admin. offices and technical service centres or entertainment for the workers.

There were no high buildings. Sylvan designers did not like heights. Most of the structures stood only ten floors. But there was a difference. Unlike anywhere in the Universe, Sylvan planets were a mystery to the eye. Everything moved. The very fabric of the offices, the technical centres, the theatres. No normal laws of matter presided. Everything moved. The mysterious art of molecular restructuring was everywhere to see or not to see. Steeleye watched. Steel beams traversing one structure to another wavered before the eyes. The one beside him as the cab halted could have been supporting any one of three buildings. The roofs above were sometimes the floors below. The doors changed places with one another in a merry confusing dance of uncertainty.

Like a time and motion study the Sylvans had mastered the art of molecular co-operation. For a stranger without body-motion techniques, the roads and pavements swayed and twisted under his feet, throwing him into a confusion of balance at every step. But a Sylvan could control the rhythm of his movements in perfect unison with the matter around him. Like a harmonising madrigal, the physical changes in the bodies of the people, particularly on the Sylvan Complex, moved delightfully in time with the slipping and sliding of the structures they had built. The zenith of sophistication, movement of matter within itself. All matter seemed to have life; all solid objects, if you did not appreciate their individual rhythms, could leap up and take a swipe at you. An adult Sylvan would never trip, never collide, rarely if ever break an object in his hands, even though it might appear to be sliding through his fingers.

Their appreciation of molecular restructuring, or co-operation between diverse matter, was supreme and so well practised that they thought nothing of it, nothing at all.

Steeleye looked around him from the cab window, which itself altered shape to seem like a reflecting pool: stones cast into it, rippling through its breadth, altering the outside patterns beyond its natural depth still further giving another layer of confusion to the picture. The nearest buildings were covered in coloured designs; each design was minutely figured to melt into the next with every movement, so that the effect was of a steel kaleidoscope of colours, no mixture of design ever creating a dull or dreary pattern, every change a new wonder of delight and beauty.

Along another muddled block stood a curved series of structures, some wavering forty feet in height, apparently changing from a perfect oval to sharper soft curves, breaking up their pattern again in the space of a few seconds to form a battlement of squares. Below the top levels of the building were windows, but only for a second, for the opaque, sepia squares changed to faces, a row of ten, highly coloured facial configurations, one smiling, another grimacing, one laughing, another crying, each one a motion of change and an emotion of lively caricature. Never a dull moment, for the design would alter again and again, probably never forming the same picture twice in its lifetime. Tourists stared, amazed, for no other planets in the Federation had this variety of display. Only the Sylvan Complex, the centre of the FUP, was so exciting, and Steeleye recorded it all, pleased by what he saw but confused that so disciplined a race could be capable of such fluid beauty.

The ground cab reflected the motions of the road under it, and better than a perfectly controlled suspension system it rode on air, a fraction of an inch above the sliding and twisting ground, changing its own shape to compensate everything below. There were open squares, closed green gardens, artificial plants and real growing fruits on trees about the centre. There were upper walkways that gave a picture of the city across several miles and underground shopping centres filled to profusion with all the goods you could ever wish to buy. A thoroughly well replenished consumer society, a living paradise for the tourist and shopper alike.

Steeleye credited the ride and exited to face a Sylvan official.

"What is your planet?"

"Cathandramis."

"Show me your papers."

Steeleye handed over Tarash's documents, attempting to control his fears, projecting mild body-motions that would not over betray his nervousness.

"Tarash eh?"

"Yes."

"You are not scheduled any leave from the Vegitators." The official past his sweeping hand across the miniature computer link attached to his belt. "In fact, you have had all the leave you were due this year. Why are you taking more, Tarash?"

"Special benefit . . ., sir, to visit my brother on Anchor, sir, they said I had better come in case I don't make it to next year's vacation, sir."

"Getting old ah? Well, we had better check that little story, come with me."

Steeleye cursed under his breath and followed the official to the nearest building. They passed a number of guards without a word from the official and entered a small room which was evidently his office. It was now or never. Steeleye knew that if the official actually got in touch with Cathandramis administration they would go out and look for Tarash, and he would have to leave Anchor at once, if he could get out. He had to silence this Sylvan quickly but not cause an alarm.

If he tried to fake an identity he might get away for a

while, but he would be discovered eventually. If he simply killed the guard he would have to get out without being stopped, and any way they would have a record of his identity from the entrance cameras which all official buildings used.

"All right, I give up, I'm not on official vacation, I'm not supposed to be here, but if you report me they'll take away my pension and that'll be it. I've got a wife still and she's very sick, she'll die if I lose my pension. Let me have my vacation and see my brother, just a day or so that's all. I promise I'll not get into any trouble and no one will know that you let me go."

"Hm, I thought you were up to no good."

"I'm not up to no good, I promise, I'm only here to see my brother and then I've got to get back quick in case my sick wife needs me. Don't report me, please."

Steeleye prepared to kill the guard, if he did not give way. He kept up the façade, body-motioning in the fashion a frightened farmer might under the scrutiny of an official. The guard wavered, obviously not keen to condemn this old Sylvan to a jail or a last few months of poverty and misery, but not keen either to get himself into trouble. Steeleye braced himself. Little did the official know that he was making a choice between his own life and death.

"Very well, but only for a day, mind. You make sure you're on that teleporter back to Cathandramis tomorrow or I'll report you, right?"

"Yes, sir, of course, sir, thank you very much."

"Well, what are you waiting for?"

"My papers, sir, and a disc for entertainment and food, sir."

"Entertainment? I thought you were going to see your brother."

"I am, sir, but he doesn't get home from work until much later and I'm too old for wandering the streets, sir."

21

"Too old for the kind of entertainment in this city . . . very well. You wish a tour."

"On Anchor, yes. But now a show, and sleep later."

"Your baggage will tansport. Come with me."

An adept at body-motion, as were all Sylvans, could change before your eyes. His whole body and face could become whatever you pleased. For the Sylvans were also systems experts. A Sylvan could detect and understand any system presented to him, however complex – even the nervous system. Like an Exonic computer he could recognise a pattern in anything. And yet with all this bizarre impermanence they were always one thing: attractive. With their legendary arrogance they would never face you with a bad face or turn on you with a bad turn. Always handsome, always beautiful. They knew what you liked the moment they met you and gave it to you in varying forms throughout the interaction, until they turned away, and then they were something else.

The official led him to a desk. It was smooth-topped at first, but once he operated its other side, small thin lines of coloured lights raced across its surface.

"What kind of show?"

He knew he must not seem too certain of himself, a touring farmer would not have been to Sylva often. But that was not difficult. Because he wasn't certain at all.

"Magic, spectacular, magic." Timion had said go to see a magician. Sylva has the best of them.

"Actual's in town, you want to see Actual?"

Steeleye hesitated, Tarash hesitated. Now they were amongst people again and queues formed behind him in seconds; there were other tourists, plenty of other tourists.

"Answer?" The official spoke in the sharp Sylvan fashion.

"Yes, fine, Actual."

He formed a shape across the board and lights darted through unseen channels, wavering as the board itself wavered. A small disc emerged.

"Press this behind your ear. It will guide you to the show. Time is yours. Until tomorrow, remember. The next in line approached and Steeleye was alone again. "Time is yours." The words he would hear on a thousand occasions, meaningless, a dead platitude.

The central city complex was vast, disappearingly enormous. The swaying buildings, walls and surfaces came and went in a plethora of confusion. Steeleye had been trained to cope with body-motion. He could control it and correspond in the subtle language with the best of them. As Tarash he had to be less proficient, or be detected.

For a statutory moment he stopped and gaped a little at the highways and lightways, peering into the air as people came and went along the "force threads" from other planets. Out of a mist came a small body, rushing towards him, from miles away, to land comfortably at his feet and move off along a groundway or take a cab in a second of controlled speed. The Sylvans knew their planet well, could cope without confusion with movement and change as they changed and moved themselves. Steeleye could have done the same, but he would not give himself away.

And all the time the Circle watched him, noted him, without his knowledge.

He pressed the disc behind his ear and it stuck, singing silently to his brain the instructions for a show of magic.

He listened and dubiously took a groundway. The movement was slow enough to comprehend as he passed the surroundings. This was the supply planet; monitoring and organising the incoming of foods, minerals, repairs, technicians, research methods, news, all forms of the Sylvan needs from the many planets built to supply the central brain of the Empire. The buildings were marked accordingly: Department of Food, Exon Centre, Computer Parts, Technical Information and Repairs, Employ Building, Work Centre; each one huge, sprawling for ever in the distance, behind and forward.

He passed on to the pleasure centres and entertainment sections in that part of the Complex. Here it was like a nightmare and a soft dream all in one. Great spans of multi-coloured lights dashed across the air. Once visions flashed before the eyes and were gone for ever. Nothing repeated.

"Canny Centre came and went. Bring your thoughts within our tent. We will cull your future ways, come let us unsort the maze."

"Breathe a wish of any size, nothing wanted but a prize. Canny Centre has the gift, any thought that we can sift."

A crack of light wielded through a huge wall of dullness and a sinuous, lithe body twisted into shape across the sky. A dancer, motioning with all the sexual movements peculiar to the Sylvans, wriggled and swirled before Steeleye. Her gestures were obvious, disturbing, almost malevolent, but beckoning. Not for Steeleye, not here.

"The psychoanalysis of thought is the complexity of mind. The complexity of mind is the brain child of the Sylvan. We can help you, from whatever race, creed or world within the Federation. If you have a problem, do not pass us, we are willing, time is yours."

The psycho-centres were well known, expensive but effective. You have a problem? Go to Sylva Six and have it sorted. All part of the amazing Sylvan systems. But like everything on Sylva, protected by movement. Everything moved.

Steeleye weaved and turned like a bewildered firstcomer to a world of polymaths. The magic of Sylva is the magic of the Universe. Steeleye knew it, but Tarash did not, and for now Steeleye was Tarash.

If the administrative areas of the Sylvan Complex planets are exciting, then the entertainment centres are a supreme indulgence of exaggeration and colour. Nothing by half measures. Throw a million colour variations into the air in a random selection and allow them to fall to the ground, forming their own unrepeatable pattern, and you might get a flash of the Sylvan facility for performance.

Over an area of some three square kilometres in the centre of Sylva Six's main city was a sprawling paradise for the rich and bored. Nothing was left unturned, no means for enjoyment unexploited: from gambling on the "Wheeler-wheels" through fabricated mystery tours into forbidden worlds of unimagined delight where you might be swallowed up into a fake tour of the Universe; you might disappear into the bowels of a home-made hell; walk through fire unharmed; jump a hundred feet into the air and land without a bruise; you could perform gymnastics like a professional, run at the speed of a champion and remain untired; make love with Ran Pef, the Sylvan lover of all time; see a hundred armies fighting the Cao wars; feature in a full-scale movie as the star; learn the language of the Kalks in a minute; pilot a battle cruiser; die and be reborn; hunt the Jarmin; take part in an orgy of discussion with the great dead philosophers, Camin, Weltor Meben; take home packets of precious stones; eat yourself to engorgement; or simply watch, listen, wonder.

For the Sylvan entertainment centres were to be seen to be believed. Steeleye wandered through the maze of this unfamiliar world, breathless at the endless variations on the same theme of fun and games for everyone, until he reached the place of his choice.

"Actual comes, Actual goes, no one knows what Actual knows."

"Here on Sylva Six, Actual gives his magic to you. Any time you choose he is here or there, or everywhere.

Enter now and be not sure, you may see him, you may not. Try a glimpse of the greatest magician in the Universe, for a glimpse is all you may get."

Steeleye entered. The disc behind his ear quietened.

Actual enjoyed a unique reputation throughout the Federation. He was surrounded by rumour, gossip and intrigue. No one knew from whence he came, or where he vanished, sometimes not returning for several months. He would be performing in the theatres and street stalls every night for weeks on end and suddenly be gone, nowhere to be found. His magic was uncanny. In an age when almost any Sylvan in the street could alter his appearance totally, when normal people could appreciate and perform complex trickery with their bodies and minds, when most living creatures had deliberate control over their molecular structure, Actual was supreme, unparalleled, beyond understanding.

Ask a passer-by to describe him and you will get a thousand different answers. Try to form a system into his facial structure and you will go crazy with the effort. The Sylvans knew systems like a farmer knows his land, but no one knew Actual. Tonight he was to perform at the Caroura Club, the best on Sylva Six, and the audience was packed. Timion had told Steeleye: "Go and see Actual, he is the best." So now, together in this unlikely place were the two most significant characters in the history of this colossal Empire, perhaps in the history of the Universe. And no one knew.

"Are you alone, sir?"

"Near the front."

"Yes, sir, come with me."

Steeleye was led across the floor and placed at a table only a few rows from the front of the auditorium. It did not occur to him that such a privilege would hardly be accorded to a common farmer. It should have occurred to him.

He sat and waited, silent with the expectant audience.

After a few minutes a small glow appeared at the centre of the stage. The glow grew larger, still larger, until it flamed slightly. There was no heat, but the flames grew higher, leaping across the centre stage, growing each second until they lifted into the air, rising to the height of a Sylvan. Still there was no heat, only the flashing glow of the fire as it reached out across the floor, seeming to touch the audience. The front rows backed away, expecting to be burnt, but there was no singe, not even a slight warmth. Steeleye felt his heart pound.

Slowly a shape materialised out of the flames. Very slowly, as in the old stories of the Phoenix, a body began to live within the flames. The shape was at first doubtful, amorphous, tenuous, but obvious to those who watched. Piece by piece the form changed from a flaming, writhing mystery into a recognisable being. The shadows from the fire died down. The shifting, heatless puzzle formed into a real living shape. As the body came, so the fire went, until only a halo of flame engulfed the form of a cloaked black figure.

With a single turn the figure swirled its cloak, and wings formed. The body was aquiline, with huge thick legs and a powerful brooding shape. The head was beaked, the wings three metres across, flapping wildly on the stage. No wind, no gusts of air emitted from the huge, frenzied limbs. The creature seemed to have complete control of its surroundings, as though it might dash the theatre to the ground and pick it up in the glimpse of an eye.

The form changed again, from bird to ape, slowly, hugely, turning around behind the cloak and re-emerging in its new form. The likeness to the primitive creatures of the ancient past was terrifying, as real as a 4D image, but sweating, smelling, roaring with total authenticity. The audience reeled back from the creature's great howl of disdain and some retched at the alien and overpowering smell. And then, as suddenly as it had

27

begun and without so much as a sound or a movement, the ape was a Man.

Man was dead in the Universe, remembered but dead, long gone, extinct. Actual had never before been known to body-motion a Man. Why did he do it now?

Immaculately dressed in white tuxedo and black bow tie he stood before his audience, cane in hand, and bowed delicately. When the chatter of amazement had died down, he spoke.

"This is a very special performance, for there is one in our midst who means much to me, and may one day mean much to us all, for better for worse.

> "But now is not the time to tell,
> The rich will fall, the poor know hell.
> Now is not the time to spy,
> Some will live and many die.
> History changes day by day,
> Powers stand and slide,
> Worlds advance and skies decay,
> Who's to say, who's to say?
> Not I, no not I."

And Actual was gone.

Steeleye knew that the reference had to be to him. How could this strange magician know so soon, how could he know? The hairs on the back of his neck stood up and small beads of sweat broke out on his forehead. Suddenly it seemed that everyone stared at him.

A rapid move now would give him away. He had to sit it out until he could leave easily. He had to give it a few moments, in the hope that Actual would return and continue the show with other tricks that meant nothing.

Moments seemed like an age. The seconds passed and a still, expectant silence dominated the auditorium. Steeleye could not control the fear any longer and he turned his head. Behind him, flanking his table, stood three Sylvan guards, tall and armed with the disrupters so familiar to their opponents. They were devastating weapons. One blast from the muzzle simply disintegrated any body or structure. Steeleye's mind raced. At the door there were at least ten more guards. How could they have known him? No one knew him yet. He must have made a false move, he must have done something. Perhaps Tarash had given the alarm, perhaps someone had warned of his coming. All these thoughts flashed across his brain in a split second as his eye began to glow. Slowly the steel hue of his right eye changed colour; slowly and then suddenly the intensity splashed a ghastly heat across the vista of his sight. The eye was hideous. In the face of a living creature one eye was clear, sharp, deadly red. The three guards before him dropped to the ground, fried, burnt to a cinder. The chairs and table behind them were scorched with the burning rays emitted from that most deadly of weapons given to him by his makers, the Eumigs. Timion had told him: "If there is trouble, use your eye, and never underestimate its power. In that eye you have the strength to burn up a fleet of battle launches, with a single glance you can stop a battle robot, disturb the whole foundation of a building. Use it with care."

Steeleye leapt to his feet and with one huge stride he traversed the gap between him and the stage. Once there he turned and sent a searing gash across the guards rushing toward him, clearing clean spaces between their heads and shoulders. One sweep of his great head was enough. The red firing ray cut through the bodies of his would-be captors like a meat axe through butter. But that was not to be the end. The Sylvans were not about to let this fish wriggle free without a fight. A single guard entered the auditorium, by now filled with the panic of a terrified audience, all dashing for the exits, prevented from their own escape by guards at every door. Everything moved and turned as the atmosphere of terror swept through the building. Only Steeleye was calm. His mighty body, built by experts for battle, strong beyond imagination, logical and clean cut, never meant for panic, stood welded to the ground, the eye blazing with death, waiting for the next onslaught.

The single guard levelled a Zonal Catheter at Steeleye's body. Had the guard been given the opportunity to use the weapon Steeleye's body would have drained of its life blood in seconds, leaving only a heap of flesh, but his mind was too sharp, his senses too alert. He caught the tense grip of the guard's mind as he prepared to attack with the Catheter. The Sylvan hid his body behind a support at the back of the auditorium. The deadly eye might not have found its aim quickly enough, and Steeleye's body was vulnerable in the centre of the stage. With speed bewildering to those still watching, he swept across the rows of tables and chairs, darting in and out, weaving back and forth, making the guard's aim impossible. As he went he displayed a little of his own magic. Employing the body-motion skills inherent in his structure he altered size, shape and meaning, taking a low, smooth form which slithered like a snake through the escaping Sylvan audience. Reaching the space where the guard still stood, watching for his quarry, Steeleye drew up to his full height and without warning sent a single streak of fire from his head, levelling the Sylvan guard to the ground. In a three-step movement he turned and knocked out two other groups of guards; turning again, he lifted another in his huge hand, dashing his helpless body against the wall.

That was the last of the living aggressors; now it was time for the big boys, and they were not far behind. Steeleye's sense had warned him early on that the Sylvans would soon recognise the inequality of the first series of attacks. They had seen this fearsome creature trample two dozen guards in the few blinks of his terrible eye. One single moment passed. Bodies lay strewn across the tables and floor. No one moved for fear of attracting that noble head in their direction. Silence fell again but only for a second and then, moving with the swiftness of racing stallions, came the Sylvan Guardians – the robots. The only mechanical robots that the Sylvans allowed on their planet were killers; armed and built to do battle, these robots stood three metres high, taller than Steeleye himself, and carried weaponry to make an army of Sylvans seem like planet ramblers. Three entered the theatre together, two weaved across the space allowed, cutting down one Sylvan after another in their mad eagerness to get across from Steeleye and cut off his retreat. The third made straight for its target, guns blasting at all levels. Its body was immense, thundering at massive speed. The challenge to a yet untried Steeleye frightened even him.

On the principle that a living mind is faster than anything mechanical, Steeleye lifted his body from the ground, swinging his legs up to the top of the support behind which had stood the Catheter guard. The first robot was not slow, however, and adjusted in a split second to tally the movement. But fast though it was, Steeleye was faster, swinging across the higher level, clearing the robot as it approached and turning in the air, concentrating his eye power to its maximum level. The ground below the robot was a hole, the robot non-existent, gone, disintegrated, no more.

The other two hesitated not one second, firing at every range into which Steeleye's body moved. They approached, but suddenly their target was not there. He had vanished from their view. Like two foolish comedians they turned to gaze at one another, as if searching for answers. And before time turned, Steeleye was behind them both. The right-hand one fell to the ground, reeling under the blast. The second took a blast to the chest but fought to come on. Steeleye played with this colossus, taunting its skill, holding it back as a long-armed boxer holds his opponent off. The robot, programmed only for attack, kept coming, thrusting its massive body against the tempered rays flooding more slowly now from the deadly eye. The ray cut off, the robot crashed to the ground, lifted, swung forward and with an aimless blow struck out with its powerful arms, flailing at the Man, missing the ducking figure. Almost a show again, almost an entertainment. The robot stood before Steeleye; for the only time in its existence it hesitated, glowering with a shadow of disbelief at this living creature that could conquer with ease such machines built for war. Triumph in his eye, Steeleye stepped forward, wrapped one muscled arm about the neck of the robot and twisted its head off.

With the ensuing pandemonium came Trok: Trok the leader of the Security forces on Sylvan planets. Trok had watched and knew that this Man had to be stopped. He levelled a simple atom blaster at Steeleye's body and pressed the trigger. The thin-edged beam blurted from the muzzle. It reached across three-quarters of the gap and stopped. Everything stopped. The darting, fearful audience ceased all movement, the quelling guards froze in their tracks. Trok's arm remained level, the blaster stilled its death ray. All was still, perfectly soundlessly still. Steeleye turned and wondered. This was not his doing.

"You fight well, my friend."

Actual stood beside him, surveying the scene of devastation.

"Needlessly it seems. What have you done?"

"A simple trick. I'll teach it to you one day. Come."

Actual led Steeleye out through the burnt and cindered theatre, past the broken battle robots, out into the clear air. Everything was still.

They entered a ground car, which moved off without so much as a word from Actual. The theatre flashed into the distance behind them.

Chapter 3

"The Lull" was a period of time named by the historians who reviewed the centuries of Sylvan rule. It extended between the ninety-fourth century and the ninety-ninth. Also known as the "Nine Hundreds" it formed the most peaceful and most repressed section of the Sylvan empirical leadership. As a phenomenon of history it is unique. No other power in the civilised Universe has ever before or since achieved such a degree of calm. But the calm was deceptive. Far below the surface were rumblings of discontent. Like the touch paper of a damp fuse, the small, dull, red glow was there and only needed one more spark to fire it.

But the sophisticated and highly evolved Sylvans had no effective opponents, and the only real trigger that fired the spark into an explosion came purely by accident.

"Surely, a little healthy competition . . .?" Hamgar leaned in the doorway.

"Healthy competition nothing, I don't need it."

"Going alone?"

"A logical assumption, Hamgar; your first for a while, I think."

If an Android could sigh, Hamgar did.

"The most significant opportunity given to us Creature Scientists in the time allotted to us, and you have to take the full credit . . ., of course."

"You amaze me."

"A chance for us to co-operate at last, and you refuse all help."

"Correct again."

Pause for further consideration.

"What if you don't make the time limit? The schedules are tight."

"Little chance of that."

"The Sylvan High Council meets in seven weeks, and the task must be completed by then."

"You astound me, Hamgar, more with each presentiment."

"Your sarcasm does you no credit, Tousle. As Chief Creature Scientist you have a great responsibility to the Eumigs, to Zrost, and you flout my suggestions, you pour contempt upon my reputation, and you treat me like a foolish lifer."

Tousle straightened from his task, turned to Hamgar and faced him squarely. "Timion has given the experimentation and creation of the Woman to me, Hamgar. He has stated that I only shall be responsible for the task in hand, for its initiation, continuation and completion, without aid or advice from you or any other Eumig. I have no need or wish for help from you, and I would be eternally grateful if you would leave me to my labours without further interruption. My gratitude to you for this small regard. Good day, Hamgar." With this Chief Creature Scientist Tousle returned to the PAL at his side and continued with the experiment.

"So you won't let me help?" Hamgar tried a soft approach.

"No!" came the hard reply.

Like two argumentative children, Tousle and Hamgar parted company, neither prepared to give way to the other. Of course Tousle was correct. The building of the Woman was his privilege, and not Hamgar's. Clause 324 of the Sylvan Federation Code was drafted to prevent the Eumig's entry to the FUP: "No creature shall become a member of the Federation unless life is proven to exist by natural causes through organic procreation on that planet of its people." The Eumigs were Androids, albeit highly evolved, but still mechanical creatures

34

without need or ability to procreate by organic means. Each Eumig thrived without much care for the best part of a million years, but membership of the Federation would be useful to them, providing them with the means to advance beyond their small planet, so far removed from the rest of the Universe, giving them a chance to extend their influence and realise ambitions spoken of only in the privacy of their political chambers.

The Federation demanded a child, a child born of a mother. So, logically, they must produce a mother to bear the child and satisfy Clause 324. They chose a race now extinct in the Universe but once the occupant of their planet and master over their kind: Man. Books and films, tapes and records of Man were left in their archives, giving exact details of his anatomy. So here too the answer was logical: build a Woman. And this was Tousle's task. Not Hamgar's.

But Hamgar was a determined and slightly ill-balanced Eumig. Many said that early battles in the Eumig sector of the Universe had damaged his circuitry and left him a little untrue to his kind. A crazy robot, but as talented as all his kind, quite capable of building life.

Thwarted by Tousle he had but one alternative: to deceive and beat his senior Creature Scientist. To take the information so closely guarded within Tousle's laboratories and complete his model first. And here was the accident.

"Subject: cerebral cortex, cerebellum, hypothalamus, stem. Session 767. PAL confirm readiness."

"PAL ready." The Phototronic Activated Liaison, or PAL, was the Eumig's scientific tool, connected by telepathic insinuation to the brain of the master and capable of most routine work. Like a ministering nurse it rushed around the laboratory, supplying instruments and assistance where required. Functioning through TI transmissions and floating on multiple force fields, it formed one of the most adaptable machines in the Universe. Yet another of the Eumings' inventions. Tousle's PAL was adapted for his rather special needs in the work of a Creature Scientist and carried delicate and precise feelers that could perform sensitive surgery.

"Suture replace laminectomies, lobe connection completed. Central lobe correspondence under test . . . now. PAL conduct."

"Confirmed. Slight irritation from trigeminal nerve. Adjust instructions awaited."

"Ready section six-ten, adjust."

"Ready."

"Report."

"Condition localised and cured."

Tousle's techniques were scientific and methodical – each part of the subject was tested and retested.

"Check records for race comparison."

"Check."

"Detail: spinal sections. Medulla oblongata."

"Ready."

Such was the dialogue in the house of Tousle. Some miles away, however, matters progressed faster and on less efficient lines.

"Corneal correction 146 commence."

"Lateral geniculate body adjust, fraction intake point 99."

"Confirmed, doubtful activity, second eye nonfunctional."

"Remove and reset lateral conjunctive centre."

"Incorrect assumption, lateral conjunctive section uncorrectable, suggest . . ."

"I am not interested in your suggestions PAL, follow instructions. Remove second eye and replace as follows . . ."

"Irreconcilable assumption, second eye must correlate . . ."

36

"Stand aside you stupid lump of Barrier . . . I'll do the job myself."

The PAL moved back in a series of rather uncertain swerves as its master blundered forward, almost knocking the machine out of force.

Hamgar had set his personal controls at top level, had secured his laboratory exits and charged about the room like a whirlwind. The PAL, set to obey his instructions, was scarcely able to keep up with the rapid series of orders. Like an almost invisible blast it raced across the experiments and controls on the main console, correcting and re-correcting in an attempt to satisfy the mad scientist robot. Hamgar would achieve something, and it would be living, so help him, living and better than Tousle's. There was little time. The Eumig Council was set to meet soon, and then on to Sylva for the final decision.

"PAL institute repairs to Hamgar central circuitry. Set for absolute rate." Hamgar had blown a few circuits on his own back trying to get the job done. Like an electronic diagram the PAL worked through its master on its master, wildly careering about, attacking Hamgar's back, pulling out circuitry wiring, adjusting the minutely detailed layout systems in an attempt to keep up with the robot's movements.

Catral elements flew across the laboratory, circuits came and went. "Paetle" equipment saw light for seconds and vanished into the body of one or other of the many pieces under construction or repair.

In the centre of it all only one thing was actually out of place. A Eumig eye, made from Barrier steel, the strongest in the Universe. The eye should not have gone where it did, but there was no time, no time.

Hamgar cursed violently, forcing his computers to accept a scientific anomaly. Thanks only to the accuracy of a logical robot brain, the body of the creature under construction was perfect in every way but that one.

"Secure exits PAL, I want to conduct these verbal tests without interruption." Tousle lifted the limp body from the bio-chamber in which most of the work had been completed. Like a giant carrying a child, he moved easily across the lab and, erecting a force body rest, set her down again, comfortably placed, quite naked in the arms of the air.

Her body was some two metres in height, slim, long-legged and warm coloured, living but sleeping still until Tousle chose to awake her for the first time. Her hair, silken and dark, fell about her shoulders, styled in a way still popular at the death of her kind, in measured tresses, heavily curled and crimped about the neck. A smooth neck, long and fine, supporting a noble head. The head of a brightly intelligent female, set broad at the forehead and rounded at the back, small nosed and large-eyed, her mouth wide and her chin perfect. The substantial features of a beautiful woman, sensuous and strong, with a determined brow and dimpled chin. The heavily lidded eyes remained closed against a strange world already familiar to her educated brain, a brain functioning at over eighty per cent of its capacity, a level never achieved by her own race. The human race, long extinct, was now recreated by robots, built by the genius of a mechanical Android, a gentle giant.

Her arms lay still at her sides, long and strong, from shoulders broad enough to sustain a life but also carry beauty. The hands folded slim and were well padded; the fingers were long, spatulate, perfectly shaped; the palms aesthetic, untroubled. The slim torso enclosed the pink organs of a new life, working yet slowly but built to withstand high strain. The skin was toughened and strong but soft and gentle; each curve of her body was authentic, sculptored by a master. Her collar bones stood out in right form, sloping down to high full breasts, ready for feeding the child so much desired by the Eumigs. The nipples, slightly pink and brown hued, swelled large at the head of their sensuous mounds, each breast sloping away to the small neat rib cage with the delicate tensile skin. The stomach lay flat across the navel, slid down against the air to the pubic mound, soft-covered with the small triangle of silken curled hair, black and thick, protection against who knows what. Each curve was absolutely in keeping, the buttocks standing out slightly, not too flat. But there was no man, or no Man, in plan. Such a waste. Such a beautiful Woman without any Man to tell her of her beauty. No matter to Tousle. This was his creation, a scientific art form upon which he now looked, waited, watched.

Tousle had built many creatures in his long life as a Creature Scientist but none so important, nor indeed so beautiful, as this one. She had taken almost a year to perfect, for her body tissue and complex organs were difficult to culture with accuracy and absolute precision. Tousle had expended more care and energy on the creation now lying before him than on anything in his abs. Like a brilliant sculptor he had caressed every curve and formed every organ to perfection. The Eumig Council would be pleased, Timion would be pleased, and Hamgar would be furious. Without help he had performed his ordained task and now it was complete at last.

"Wake her, PAL."

The small sweeping disc passed over her head and touched the brow with a kiss. Her eyes opened. Without moving her head a fraction she allowed her eyes to roam the lab. With wide, even sweeps she took in her surroundings, gathering the maximum information with every turn. Still keeping her head quite still she passed over the PAL and then Tousle. As she watched the Eumig before her, her hands lifted and slowly passed across her body, smoothing over each change in shape, caressing the ways and means of her life, sliding through each form, without looking, without taking her eyes from Tousle, until the tour of discovery was completed. Then she spoke.

"Is there a mirror?"

Her soft, low voice uttered the words with such assurance that Tousle hesitated for a second. The PAL picked up the message and set up a reflector before her body, sweeping one feeler across the air and diverting the atoms to suit her needs. The tour began again. This time the arms remained still and the eyes took in each shape, searching once and then again, turning the corners of her body without comment. Tousle watched her pupils, watched them enlarge slightly, absorbing the light of her own form and finally returning to his face once again.

She watched him for some long time, passing her gaze only about his head and shoulders appreciating, again without comment or surprise, the difference between his appearance and her own. Then she lifted her body and stood before the moving reflector, controlled by the obliging PAL. Each muscular effort was reported to her eyes. She swung her arms, lifted her legs one by one, turned her head, swayed her hips, bent her back, tossed her hair, touched her face. Each and every response, already known, was tested for authenticity, tried for trust and worthiness. Seemingly satisfied, she turned to Tousle.

"It is strange. I have spoken only four words and yet I know so much. I have lived only minutes and yet I am aware of many hours. My mind seems to have knowledge without experience. I have no memory but I remember everything before I lived. I understand each and all the ways of my body and mind and yet nothing touches me from outside. I can see sights I have not seen, I can conjure pictures I have not passed, I can find each part of me and name it, see each part of you and believe it to be there, and yet I am just born."

"That is correct."

"And you are my creator."

"Indeed."

"You leave open your mind for me to see. You let me in on your thoughts, your amazing circuits, your vast knowledge. I feel trust."

"This is intended. Your life is new and you must not fear your surroundings. You are quite safe here and we wish that you should be relaxed and unafraid. You may have whatever you wish. The PAL will read your instructions, spoken or unvoiced, and supply every need you have."

"I am the only Woman here, aren't I?"

"Yes."

"You will not build another human."

"No, we do not intend it."

She fell silent.

"Is there some problem?"

"I feel very lonely."

"But we are here . . . there are thousands of us on this planet and we all wish to help you, make you happy."

"But there is no human, nothing living."

"Not on Zrost."

"No."

"You show signs of sadness, strong waves of sadness. I am sorry that this is so. I had not calculated that it should be."

"I think that you cannot calculate everything, Tousle."

"No, so it would seem. What would you suggest?"

"I was built by you. Why not build another?"

"That is not possible. We need only one. But you will give birth to another."

"By artificial means, not natural means."

"That is so."

"I don't like that much."

"What difference does it make? The result will be the same."

"No."

"Explain."

"The child will be made through . . . through chemistry not nature."

"The two are the same. A Man-child is made through chemistry, the chemistry of the body – your body. The seed is merely injected by a Man. This is the way it was. Even in the later times of Man, artificial insemination amongst humans was common."

"I wish it could be different."

There was silence for a moment.

"I am cold," said the Woman.

"Do you wish that I should increase the heat?"

"No, I wish clothes."

"But we are to test your body, and it would be quite different with covering.

"Nevertheless I wish not to be naked."

"Why?"

"Because . . . because you are able to see me."

"That is indeed logical."

"It may be logical, it is also . . . not what I wish."

"You cannot always have what you wish."

"But you said I could."

"We must experiment, see the reactions of your body. What harm can there be in my seeing you naked for that purpose."

"I have no privacy. I am born into a strange world able to do all the things that would normally take years to learn, but I am still naked, like a newborn baby. You do this to me and expect me not to react in the way that I have."

"I am sorry, I do not understand."

"I am an adult, I am a Woman, from the race of Man. I have feelings of insecurity, I need the comfort of privacy.

"Embarassment in front of a metal machine?"

"You display all the features of life."

42

"But you know that I am not alive."

"Nevertheless, unless you give me some clothes I will first scream very loudly and then I will refuse to co-operate with your experiments.

"I see." Tousle did not see, but evidently he had little choice.

"Please hurry."

"Very well. PAL, supply suitable clothing."

The PAL obeyed without question.

"Thank you."

"Once you are clothed we will start with some simple intelligence tests."

The Woman donned her clothing quickly and expertly.

"Thank you. The clothes fit well."

"Right, would you be kind enough to answer some questions?"

"If I can."

"Certainly you can. Let us start with some simple logic. What is a propositional function?"

"A scheme such as 'X is mortal' which can be converted into a proposition by the substitution of a determined value."

"Give me an example of a subject-predicate proposition."

"Socrates is mortal."

"Good."

"Very boring though."

"Logic is essential if you are to survive in a logical world."

"Very well, continue."

"Give me an example of the logic of terms."

"Well, there is a proposition that says that there are Men, and all Men are mortal. This implies that some mortals are Men and is inconsistent with and contradictory to the fact that some Men are not mortal, which is itself compatible with the fact that some Men are mortal. Therefore no Men are mortal implies that no mortals are Men and is inconsistent with and contra-dictory to the fact that some Men are mortal."

"Good, very good. Now, then."

"No more mortality please. What's the point?"

"Logic my dear, logic, that's the point."

"But you know I know it all, like a blessed book right up to functional calculus. I can quote Paranouus to the last word – but surely I don't need to. Do I?"

"Well, all right. Let's try some universal physics."

"Very well." She sighed.

"What is the theory of time travel?"

"That all dimensions are isolated and related only to the existence of matter."

"So time travel is impossible without matter?"

"Not necessarily. It has simply not been proved that time moves as a dimension without matter."

"Who discovered time travel as a science?"

"Paranecius III."

"What is the basic theory of teleportation?"

"The logical and membered regrouping of disrupted atoms."

"Explain the 4D image."

"A 4D image is produced by the Clas crystal in a state of molecular disturbance. The computed Exon rays are pre-distributed and projected into the crystal, which plays them on to a similarly computed Exon force field. With each movement the crystal changes its distribution of the projection according to the Exon, thus giving a backward view from inside the projection and a correct view from the perimeter."

"Good, excellent even."

"Is that all?"

"Not quite, a couple more. Let's try a few random sciences."

"I can't wait."

"What is cloning?"

"The science of living tissue duplication."

"What is the basis of mind?"

"The functioning of physiological tissue over an efficiency level of fifty-four per cent."

"Who was Jesus Christ?"

"A philosopher, Jew and philanthropist of particular note who lived during the early years of Man on Earth. He was born during the year known as AD 1 and died by crucifixion in AD 33. He created the religion of Christianity, upon which Man relied for almost three thousand years as a prop to his lack of knowledge and general insecurity of existence. He was found by later time travellers to have been a highly gifted precognitive genius and in his particular gifts was not equalled until the birth of Gerontimus Galthara, the second Christ who instituted the scientific religions in the twenty-eighth century which eventually replaced Christianity in Earthly importance."

"Who was Mantua?"

"The first Multi-Man."

"What was a Multi-Man?"

"A development of genetic science which enable Men to create creatures capable of several simultaneous levels of mental capacity, the artificial reproduction of mutated genii and several forms of Animan."

"What was an Animan?"

"Part Man, part animal."

"Why did it fail as a science?"

"Because of the genetic revolutions."

"Good, you've passed."

"Of course. What did you expect?"

"You display the very Earthly characteristic of arrogance."

"You made me."

"Indeed. Now for some physical tests." Tousle motioned to her to stand.

"Shall I stand on my head?"

"If you wish, though I think it of little value."

"Not much less than the function of X as a mortal Man."

There was a great blast of sound in Tousle's ear, the warning signal of the Eumigs.

"Turn down the rating PAL, come here you stupid . . . get him off the . . ." Hamgar thrashed out at the PAL and sent it reeling across the lab. The Man stood unsteadily, rubbing his right eye, reaching out for something to steady him. "Curse the Sylvan worlds, hold him, I will have this done my way! Hold him, PAL!"

The PAL laid its tentacles across the Man's shoulders and attempted to push him back on to the couch. The strength was not enough, and the battered machine took another blow, this time from the living creature. It sank uncertainly to the ground, knocked from its force fields, defenceless.

"Stun, for the sake of Anchor stun him!"

No response.

Hamgar took two enormous strides across the lab and laid both hands on the arms of the Man. He reacted instantly, his right eye turning dull red. His huge arms strained against the vast strength of the Eumig, slowly forcing the powerful hands upwards. He swung suddenly downwards again and released the grip. Hamgar felt the burning eye, the one steel eye, the robot eye he had implanted so quickly, so thoughtlessly into the Man to save time. It was a mistake, a bad mistake. He could not retaliate, he could not damage this creature now, not at this stage, now that he had succeeded.

The Man delivered a ringing blow to Hamgar's head.

"May the gods of . . ."

The Man levelled the eye's power at Hamgar's chest, aiming instinctively for the centre of the robot's circuitry. One quick blast and Hamgar's circuits hung loose. But still that was not enough.

Hamgar reached for the main console, took a lunge for

46

the stun pistol that lay in readiness for such emergencies and levelled it at the Man's chest, fired. The first stun knocked him sideways.

"Curse my own damned cleverness, strong as a blasted space launch." A second stun and the Man fell, dragged himself up again and intensified the eye beam at Hamgar's head. Another stun and the Man fell again, still to struggle to his feet. Hamgar pressed a contact on his arm and a shrieking howl went out across the planet, a huge sonic boom that deafened every Eumig on the surface – the Zrost emergency warning, directionalised to Hamgar. Within seconds the lab doors were burst open and the Man was secured by penal beams.

"Get me another PAL, need repair fast, take the Man . . . take him to Tousle, quickly. Be careful, don't damage him, valuable, unique, don't . . ." and Hamgar lost his sense contact with the surroundings.

"You must be aware that you are here for our purposes. That we built you to help us with a project much bigger than the importance of Man."

"You are hard."

"No, I do not intend to be hard. I have created you, I do not wish you to suffer unhappiness." Tousle laid a huge hand on her shoulder. "You will grow used to our ways, you will not be lonely for long, it will pass . . ." The last words broke off as the sound crashed through Tousle's head.

"Emergency, Hamgar . . ." Tousle sped from the lab into the open and centred his mind on the emergency in Hamgar's lab. He took a visual sensing and watched the whole drama, as it happened. As he saw the Man taken he returned to the lab once more.

"It seems you may have your wishes," he said to the woman, half thinking of the consequences of what he said.

"My wishes . . . a Man? I read you, there is a Man, here on Zrost, somewhere close."

"Yes, I have built you well, you sense correctly. There is a Man, and quite a Man it seems, built by Hamgar, the foolish Eumig Hamgar. You shall see him soon. But for now, wait in here, the PAL will see to your needs."

The woman paused. "Tousle?"

"Yes?"

"You have a name, I don't."

"What shall we call you, then? I think . . . Chaos."

"But I am not chaos."

"You are to me."

Chaos left with the PAL and Tousle stood awaiting the Man. The accident had occurred, now all that could be done was to watch and wait.

Chapter 4

Now the Eumigs, in all their mechanical wisdom, had
foreseen the arrival of Chaos. They had deliberated,
discussed, debated the necessity of some living creature
to give them at least a small means by which to fulfill the
legal requirements of the Sylvans' Code. But none had
considered the coming of Steeleye. None, not even poor
Hamgar, had imagined in their complex circuitry that a
Man would soon be walking their planet. And such a
Man.

Steeleye was two and a half metres tall, broad-
shouldered and immensely strong. His features were
square set, perfectly formed and without blemish but for
the amazing eye. His nose was long and well shaped, his
mouth suitably passionate and strong, his chin slightly
dimpled, his hair thick and blond. His one real eye was
blue, green hued with a sharp look of awareness, his facial
muscles were exact and expressive, but his one steel eye
was astonishing. Slightly larger than the real eye, it fitted
perfectly in place and did not make him look grotesque;
rather it gave an impression of contained power. His look
would turn upon you and with a lazy confidence the steel
eye would stare without blinking, while the other would
move in normal fashion.

Behind the eye was a tight circuitry of power threads,
completely independent of the rest of the body and
containing a heat ray disturber which could emit so much
power that it could crumple and burn a fleet of speeding
launches. In one small two-inch-square cavity behind
the orb lay the development of which the Eumigs were
most proud – the miniaturised blaster. It was more

49

powerful and devastating than most hand blasters used by the Sylvans and, being situated in the eye, had the advantage of surprise. The heat given out from this eye did not affect the surrounding tissue in the head, and the vast atomic blast caused not even the slightest discomfort to the owner.

His legs were huge, his arms thick and well shaped, his hands long and sensitive but firm and strong-gripping. He was taller, stronger, more dangerous, more self-willed, more loving, more ambitious than any Man had been when Man lived. An extraordinary Man, the only Man. The Eumigs were fascinated, and poor Chaos was a little overshadowed.

But she objected not at all, for there was a companion of her own type, a Man.

Hamgar had performed a rapid, haphazard but extremely impressive task in the construction of Steel-eye.

"Well, the unexpected Man."

"Yes, I feel a little unwelcome too."

Tousle sat before Steeleye and Chaos in his laboratories. "The unexpected is always unwelcome, especially to an Android. You are not part of the plan, you are therefore not logical to us. However, I must give Hamgar his credit, he has built you well, apart from that eye."

"I would not know of its existence if I did not look in a mirror. I see through it as well as the real eye, I can extend its lens much further than that of the other eye, and it evidently contains weaponry that would be useful to me."

"How?"

"Well, there are tasks to be undertaken, I think."

"Such as?"

"The Sylvans. You wish to rule the Federation, I will help you."

"Single handed?"

"Certainly. What makes you think I cannot?"

"Because the Sylvan Empire is vastly strong, enormously powerful. We would not presume to launch an attack on them, and we are 60 000 strong."

"But you are robots."

"So?"

"I am a Man. I will lead you."

"I see."

There was silence. Tousle, being a robot, was prone not to become excited by emotions. He did not feel irritated by arrogance, he did not feel amused by conceit such as this, but he knew the feelings. He knew that they would have been appropriate had he been a lifer. "You realise that you may bring danger to us by attacking the Federation."

"Certainly, but there is no accomplishment without some danger or risk. And you do want to take a greater part in the management of Sylva, do you not?"

"Perhaps."

"Well, you won't do it with a child, of that you may be sure."

"And you would wish us to release you to such a task?"

"I will not live if you do not release me, for I shall die in the attempt."

"Why?"

"Why not?"

"I would imagine an Earth Man to call that reply a feeble reason for risking your and our lives."

"I am ambitious, idealistic, strong. I am not about to sit around within the paradise of Zrost and contemplate my navel."

"That I understand. You seem to have an excess of energy, thanks to Hamgar, but there is no need to rush, my friend. A little planning would stand you in good stead."

"I have made my plans. First I must take a disguise, and visit the Sylvan Complex."

"Hmm, the problems of instant knowledge. Had you been born you would have had to learn slowly."

"But I was not born. I was built and given all the knowledge that you possess, so my decisions are made immediately. I shall be departing for Sylva Six, via Cathandramis, in the morning."

"Why not go now?"

"Because I wish to learn a little of Chaos, my wife Chaos."

"So you do have compassion, love, the legendary emotions of Man?"

"I am a Man, Tousle, even with this eye I am a Man, and I may not see the only other member of my race for some while, so I would like at least to share her bed for a night."

"Of course."

Silence.

"How will you go to Cathandramis?"

"Teleport."

The night on Zrost was a long one. Darkness fell and remained for almost twelve full hours. The three distant suns providing light and heat to the Eumig world interacted in the half night and left a scattering of colours across the sky, like reflected auditors of darkness.

Steeleye stood naked at the window formed from the walls, clearing sight through matter across two surfaces and giving a broad vista of the wind-blown sky. He watched the multi-coloured air, the greened cloud clusters and the star speckles that caught the colour and reflected like a multi-hued Christmas tree.

The wind gushed across the land, sending small rushes of dust into the air to pick up still more colour refractions, making rainbows of patterned debris from the earth. The land was green here, out away from the city in their small dwelling, private and undisturbed by the thin rumbling of Eumig mechanics. For the Eumigs did not rest at night, continuing their existence at all times.

Man and Woman were given the privilege of their needs in this small outback of silent, warm, protected privacy.

At this time no one outside the Eumig planet knew of Steeleye or Chaos, and Steeleye was painfully aware that this might be the last night of his life when he could be sure of safety with the woman he loved. Through the invested knowledge in him he knew her exactly as she was and loved her for herself. There was no growth in him until now, the adulthood was imposed suddenly. There was no learning till now, only discovery of that learning. His body had never loved her body, but he knew her absolutely; every intricacy of her needs, every perfection in her form, all the attitudes of her mind, for as lovers their minds were unshielded from one another. Co-operation would be total, interaction complete, with only the slow, testing, teasing responses of two long-standing lovers who have never loved.

He turned to her and looked at the naked, clear-skinned, slightly shadowed body, knowing what he would see but knowing nothing of the experience in fact.

Chaos turned without speaking, reading his mind, and lay slowly upon the bed. Steeleye moved to her side, sitting on the edge of the bed, lowering his great noble head to rest upon her forearm, touching the slightest first touch, without presumption, without demand.

"Steeleye?"

"Yes?"

"I want you to kiss me."

Steeleye moved closer and touched his lips to hers, and as he did her body moved with the long knowledge of its art, for the first time testing the pull she had upon him. His kiss had been tender and yet asking, gentle but sure, and her body moved to encourage him. The long slim back arched smoothly, pushing forward her full breasts, which lying back formed long orbs upon her chest. Her legs moved, one lifting slightly in a sensuous question. His strong hand moved down over her and slightly caressed the gentle skin, feeling the real warmth he knew he would find, but for the first time. Slowly he moved beside her, sliding the full length of his body against hers. Their skin touched the whole length, caressing against caresses; still kissing she lifted her long leg over his muscular, resting limbs and gently took him in her hand, quietly sliding the strong erect penis into her.

The whole experience was quite new. They knew nothing of it in reality, all was discovery, all was finding and sampling something they had both been taught was delicious, but not half so delicious. Their minds open to one another and their bodies totally willing and totally honest, they indulged in love-making intensified by the knowledge that they were the only two people in their world. They were isolated and together, so that the feelings of insecurity and dependence were intermixed, and the wind blew blessings upon them, the colours of the shaded sky cast across their bodies as they moved gently and slowly in total harmony.

"Do you imagine that here could ever have been, anywhere in the history of the whole Universe, two less experienced, newly created living creatures who could make love like that?"

"It is a strange experience." Steeleye lay still, Chaos resting her head upon his shoulder.

"To know and yet not to know. To be aware before knowing. To feel what you have expected to feel, without ever having felt anything."

"I'm sure we are unique. There cannot have been anyone like us before."

"The Universe is for ever, before and after, after and before, without beginning or end. We are not unique in that sense, only in our own selves are we unique, and that is not certain."

"How can there be another Steeleye?" Chaos asked.

"There may be thousands and millions of Steeleyes. Where there is infinity, there is duplication."

"Would that I could live for infinity and know an infinite number of you."

"We have long lives, perhaps hundreds of years. We shall love many times."

"No, you will go, I will not see you for ever."

"I pledge to you, Chaos. I pledge that so long as I live you will know me in love."

They lay still, beset by a calm sadness at the inevitability of their future. Steeleye knew that he would be gone the next day, perhaps not to return for months, perhaps never to return alive. The night passed, in colour and wind, the night passed slowly.

Chapter 5

Time started, Trok's beam hit thin air, Steeleye was gone. "Clear up here, let's go." Trok rapped out the orders and departed without ceremony from the quivering theatre.

Steeleye sat still and quiet in Actual's ground car, thinking over what had just happened. Somehow this Magician had stopped time, and now had evidently started it again. Why?

Somehow Actual had known of Steeleye's existence on the planet. How? For some reason he had chosen to save his life. Again, why? If this Time Magician was really so great, so unknown, if he came and went, saving creatures like Steeleye, he would hardly be given licence to perform in the Federation again. Trok would see to that. There must therefore be some ulterior motive behind his noble act. He must need Steeleye for something, some purpose of his own.

The Magician sat, wavering in the characteristic style, slightly calmer now, his body-motions shifting only slightly as he watched the control panels of the car guide the vehicle along the high travel roads around the city and out towards who knows where. Actual was tall now, taller than most Sylvans; his features, or what could be distinguished of them, were smooth and clear, his head swathed in a colourful cloth that hung in a neat cloak about his neck and continued down, joining with his body clothing. The outfit was slightly theatrical. His legs lay comfortably stretched along the floor of the vehicle, and he spoke not a word.

This Sylvan needed further investigation. Steeleye ran his hand across the back of his head and plucked a hair from his thick, bushy, blond head, swept his hand back down again and carefully, without Actual noticing, deposited it on the clothing of the Magician. It adhered.

"Where are you taking me?"

"Away from the centre, away from Trok."

"And you?"

"I have other business to attend to. I will leave you outside the city and continue back into the centre by another route."

Silence; nothing was to be gained through conversation, and Actual had securely closed his shields against thought transmission.

"Here, Steeleye, this is where we part company. You will be safe enough for a while, but I suggest you leave the planet quickly."

"I hope we shall meet again," said Steeleye.

"No doubt we shall. Goodbye."

Steeleye left the vehicle and it sped away, Actual still carrying the thin, almost invisible hair on his shoulder.

Steeleye tuned into it with his brain receiver, for it acted as a fine transmitter, sending out signals telling where it went, wherever it went. Another ground car appeared round the corner and Steeleye concentrated his eye on the road, shooting a blast of heat out just before the car and burning up a chunk of the road, sending great billows of steam up as the materials ignited. The car stopped and the driver leapt from the seat, brandishing a blaster. Steeleye glanced at him and knocked the blaster away, stunning the driver to the ground. He climbed into the control seat and sped away after the bleeping signals from Actual. The two cars, several kilometres apart, flashed along the circular highway back into the city and Steeleye drew his machine up. Actual had docked, inside the main Sylvas building.

Here he stopped and considered the next move. "Actual has access to the Sylvas private chambers, so he must be part of their close network. He is in there now, and going gradually deeper into the lower levels." Steeleye got out of the ground car and looked up at the vast building, spreading for several hundred metres each way, to west and east.

The streets around were fairly empty, as usual. This part of the city was occupied by workers in the daytime, and very few emerged into the streets except at the end of their work shift.

It was clear daylight and the third sun sent down its bright light into the domed Complex from the north-west.

The building itself was not guarded by Sylvans, but most of the entrances forbade anyone past them, being mostly sealed off by force beams that made it impossible without passes or special authority to obtain entry to the hallowed buildings of the leaders of the Empire.

The walls swayed before Steeleye, the shape of the main entrance twisting and turning as though with the wind, and Steeleye shivered slightly as he conceived the only way in.

He checked his belt. Here he had teleport facilities which would be useless within the building without special release, and he had small rocket thrusters that could propel him over short distances, and he had a tiny hand blaster.

The arrest chutes, invisible to the eye, he knew were sunk into the ground just below the entrance point, and without a pass anyone trying to get through would be swallowed up without so much as a whisper.

"The arrest chutes, the only way. But what happens underneath?" He stood still, doubtful. He knew nothing of what they held. But he reasoned, speaking softly under his breath, as though to reassure himself.

"If passes run out, get out of date, as they must, then anyone could be swallowed up. They must make mistakes, even the Sylvans, and if a Sylvas should get caught up under there they wouldn't want him hurt. They must allow for that, they must. But where do they go? What happens when the trap doors shut? There can't be hundreds and thousands of penal centres, they must carry the body to a centre somewhere else in the city underground. That gives me time. Time to escape, time to find an entrance point down there." He pondered, but knew he had little time, for Actual was getting further and further away and sooner or later someone would spot him standing out here.

"Must get in, no alternative, have to use the chutes." He stepped forward, taking his life in his hands, not knowing what would become of him once inside the dreaded chutes. No one knew, for no one ever came out to tell the tale.

He stepped forward, touched the force field before him and the doors opened at his feet, literally grabbed at him and tugged his body down. He pulled back in a moment of panic, but the drag was too great and he was sucked under.

"Tractor beams. Heavy tractor beams, pulling me," he muttered as he went, trying to keep his cool.

"Must keep upright, can't lose equilibrium. Light, there's light. And not too much space, very tight fit." The tractor beams acted like a comforting cocoon, grasping the body in a wrap of force beams that carried the collected item on a cushion of comfort, guarding it against the surrounding walls of the chutes. His arms were bound to his sides and his body was held rigid, the beams shifting his shape to fit the area into which he fell. As if with an invisible strait-jacket, he was strapped and held against his will, and carried to an unknown destination.

"No time, thing works fast. Must get out of the tractor straps, must break free, can't use my belt." Steeleye forced his arms against the beams and managed to fight against the force, but it was a constant and exhausting battle, for the beams did not break, they merely gave under the strength exerted against them. No normal Sylvans would have possessed the strength, but Steeleye's superior size and power strained the beams and stretched their capacity. But he was moving fast and he had no time to fool around.

"Body rocket, got to fire the body rocket." He pressed the button on his belt and the small thruster blasted a tiny but effective force from behind and stopped the tractor beams' directional flow.

He felt like a floating piece of wood, a fish fighting against the force beams, belching down the tunnel like liquid from a pump. The going was hard and not helped by the constant need to keep his arms from being trapped at his sides.

"There was a door, another corridor further back. Another way through." He had seen a bend in the tunnel as he came through the chutes, which went off in another direction just near the top, and he fought to get back there.

It was impossible to grasp the sides of the tunnel, which were smooth and without any join or break in the surface. He had to rely entirely on skilful thrust from the rocket at his belt. The force kept coming, unsympathetic to his plight, pushing against his great strength like a hurricane against a giant. He seemed to make three metres and be pushed back two, and the power in the rocket would not last for ever. Let that run out, and he was finished.

"Eye force, use the steel eye, get extra power." He turned his eye to the slowly receding tunnel below him and aimed at the bending sides. Using a low power he sent out a beam of energy to thrust him harder up the tunnel, but because he had to look down to do it there was no way of telling his direction upwards. But it worked; the extra energy thrust sent him faster and easier up the tunnel towards the fork at the top, and eventually he was able to grasp the edge and pull himself up.

"Made it! Thank the Eumigs for that. Now, what's up here?' Pulling his body over the edge of the shaft he suddenly felt the force beam cut away. He was out of the main flow of tractor beams, and out of the water onto dry land. Or so it seemed. He collapsed onto the metallic surface and tried to regain a little of his spent strength.

"That was fun, that really was some fun. See if we can't avoid arrest chutes in the future. No wonder nobody ever gets out of them."

This new tunnel was wider, and short so that the dim light available from the chute below him lit a shadowed chamber in front, at the end.

"This must be a maintenance entrance. Probably leads to the control systems. I'll bet it's locked too."

He crawled, still tired from his efforts, to the clamped doorway. "Now, how do we get in here?"

He took the handle in both hands and twisted, fully prepared to counter strong resistance. But the door opened freely.

"Well, well, they really don't expect visitors."

He pushed the door open slightly, peering into the chamber, looking for guards, but there was no one in sight. "Confidence, Sylvans, can be a bad thing in large quantities." He climbed in, stealthily dropping to the ground of the large chamber. Before him and all around were the panels and control consoles for the force fields within the arrest chutes.

Steeleye looked around, checking that no one lurked inside, waiting for him with a blaster, but the chamber was quite empty. The ticking machinery buzzed and clicked around him, lights flashing the satisfactory working of the complex mechanism, evidently quite untroubled by the foreign body in their presence.

"I must be the first to have defeated an arrest chute. Hmm, one up to Steeleye. Now, where's Actual?"

He walked to the door and opened it out into a corridor, gaining no confidence from his success so far. There were bound to be security guards somewhere around.

Sure enough, outside the door were two heavily armed Sylvans pacing up and down the row of chambers across the corridor. Steeleye shut the door carefully and considered what to do about them.

"Two of them. They mustn't be allowed to call the alarm. I want to get out of this place alive. Two guards . . .' He turned and looked about the chamber. Something could, of course, go wrong with the machinery in the room. That might bring one of them in to investigate and then the other would follow if there was enough noise.

Steeleye moved across to the nearest control board and flipped a switch marked 'Force break'. There was a loud clank from outside and a small red light flashed on the panel. Another light came on outside and voices were heard from the Sylvan guards. Steeleye stood behind the door.

The first guard entered and Steeleye burnt a neat hole in the back of his neck before he could so much as breathe a word. "Hey, come and help " Steeleye muffled his voice from inside the chamber to summon the other guard.

"What's up, can't you do a simple job . . .?" and the second guard died.

"Now, a clear way through. Through where? Through here." Before him, down the corridor, were ten doors, each one marked by a number and a name, except for the tenth, which was blank. Steeleye chose this one to enter.

"Perhaps this is the home of the mighty Time Magician. He could have gone this way."

Steeleye looked about him at the beautifully decorated room, at the movi-prints on the wall reflecting and changing to the taste of the observer; at the great viewing screen on the wall and the 4D crystal unit in the corner.

At one side there was a force desk, invisibly carrying the various requisites for a working administrator, and behind that a door to the transtube. This was a private transtube connecting the occupier of the office to whatever planet in the Complex he wished to visit, and it was down here that Actual had gone.

"So, dear Actual is pretty powerful, more than a mere performer, a Sylvas even. And he wants me in one piece. Wants to find out more about me before he blows my head off or turns me into a toad. OK, Actual my friend, let's see where you have laid your trap."

Steeleye stepped into the transtube chamber and pressed the button for travel to Anchor, the central planet. This was where his quarry had gone, so why not follow, straight into the spider's web?

The room into which he emerged on Anchor was much the same as the one he had left, empty and plush, expensively decorated, smelling of some fine incense and warmed delicately for comfort and ease. There was only one difference: it had a second door. On this door was an emblazoned circle, embossed in gold and alive with colour. There had to be something worth looking at behind that. Casually, perhaps too casually, Steeleye opened the door. There was nothing to stop him. This was a privileged entrance, the entrance evidently of a very important member of the Sylvan society. Actual's entrance, unless Actual really was a magician and could use the privileges of others freely. Going into the chamber through this door was like opening the entrance to a communications booth expecting to find a small space inside and discovering instead a vast chamber. Steeleye had stepped from an ordinary medium-sized room into the most colossal, high-ceilinged anti-room. It swept away from him at least eighty metres on all sides, and the floor space was banked wall to wall with computer complexes, great expanses of control panelling video screens, telecommunications systems, interpretive monitors, reference tapes, many many features of what had to be a highly complex piece of equipment. Right at the centre stood the most dazzling feature.

Set on a podium, some three metres from the ground, hung a great circle. Like an enormous upright halo it seemed to hang without support centimetres above the podium, quite still, no wavering or shape changes. Its edge was colour hued, and about its perimeter were two large golden balls of light, both near the bottom, one on either side, spinning independently.

There was an atomosphere of power, of strength and dominance, sinister, forbidding, dangerous.

"The Centre of Power," gasped Steeleye, hesitant. What had he entered now?

He stood, dwarfed by the magnificent presence of the Circle, legs apart, staring up like a worshipping believer before a great god. There was little sound. Only the gentle humming of the computers in the background. Nothing emitted from the Circle itself, and as he stood watching, Steeleye felt insecure, losing his inherent confidence. "What do I say? Who do I speak to? What are you?"

He felt almost foolish, but there was no doubt that somewhere in the chamber was an intelligence far greater than his own. He stepped towards the podium. At the centre of the front, underneath the Circle itself, there was a pressure point, a series of question plates that would reveal information, presumably through the Circle itself. Steeleye touched the buttons.

The screen lit sharply and a picture of Steeleye himself appeared, twisting and turning in a ghastly void of dull greyness. His body seemed tormented, broken; he cried out in pain and thrashed around, overpowered by something quite beyond his control. Steeleye watched, horrified.

"What do you show me?"

"Your death, Steeleye, your death."

The picture continued until the body, now battered and broken, fell through hundreds of metres, falling into nothing, dragged through the eternity of space.

"You know of my death?"

"I am your death. You will not live beyond this chamber, Steeleye. You are a thorn in the side of the Experiment."

"I do not come here to die."

"But you will, there is nothing you can offer me, or the Sylvans. What would you have me do, free you?"

"Yes. I can help your experiment."

"How can you help something about which you know nothing?"

"You know nothing of the Eumigs." Steeleye slowly backed away from the Circle, hoping vaguely to get to the door.

"There is no way out, Steeleye." Suddenly strong beams lashed at his arms and strapped them to his sides.

"I can give you knowledge of the Eumigs. You need to know what they can do to harm you."

"Why should you do that, you who are a product of the Eumigs?"

The beams grew stronger about his body, almost slicing through his flesh. He fought uselessly, his strength of no avail against this monster of power. "I wish only power for myself."

"How will this be accomplished? What should I give you in return?"

"My life."

"I can kill you, get rid of you for ever and find the ways of the Eumigs myself."

"You have no contact with them, and if you kill me they will build another and another. They can build one, why should they not build hundreds?"

"Then I will kill hundreds."

"You will grow tired of that and each one will come

better equipped to combat your skills. I have learnt something, and my follower will know what I know."

There was silence, then the tractor beams were released.

"Go, do as you say, plant your contact between me and the Eumigs, let me see that your word is good. For if it is not, Steeleye, you will surely lose your life."

Steeleye staggered from release, moved quickly to the door and returned the way he had come, teleporting from Sylva Six back to Zrost.

Chapter 6

Coming back to Zrost was like breathing again. There was no shifting and changing, no awful uncertainty, just the simple, all embracing wisdom of the Eumigs. No arrest chutes, no security systems, no rush and bustle, only the great elegant movements of the huge robots going about their business without the twittering nervousness of sparrows. For the first time Steeleye looked upon his home planet and saw it for what it was: calm, powerful and beset with the assured strength of creatures attuned so finely to their surroundings that they needed only to sense a presence to know its motives, needed only to detect evil through any one of their systems, knowing that they had infinite capacity to deal with it, no fuss or bother.

Two smooth-moving, striding Eumigs came towards Steeleye. Timion and Tousle, looking, if it is possible, as concerned as brooding fathers. Eumig faces are equipped with tensile strength and, though their emotive responses were purely simulated by biotic tuners, they could very often seem genuinely to be 'feeling' what they showed. A small wind blew on the planet that day, a shifting, chilling wind, and Steeleye shuddered slightly as a gust caught about his strong chest.

"We are glad that you came, Steeleye. Welcome."

"Glad, very glad," Tousle added, as if to convey his evident concern.

"I have some interesting news."

"Before your news, Steeleye, we have some of our own. Chaos has gone."

"Gone? Where, for the sake of Man, where?"

"We do not know for sure. The tracking beams have hold of her movements, but they are uncertain, and I am not sure that some form of scrambling device is not shadowing their progress."

"Their? Who took her?"

"Come, walk with us." They loped in the characteristic long strides of the Eumigs, Steeleye having to step a little faster than he was accustomed to keep pace with his giant makers.

"A small launch came here from the Sylvan Complex, headed by Trok, the Security leader. He came with only five Sylvans on a peaceful errand to talk of some problem to which he alluded at length without specific mention of his true intent."

"He had suffered some severe losses in the Sylvan Guard at a theatre in the central entertainment district of Sylva Six and was concerned that we Eumigs might have access to information about the device through which three battle robots and a host of guards were destroyed without apparent effort by a powerful creature using a device with which this Trok was not familiar!" Tousle spoke with small sarcasm.

"And you did not tell him of your recent creation?" asked Steeleye.

"We thought it well to exclude ourselves from any political, or indeed extensive, involvement in the matter. We imagined that it would cope with itself without any serious interference from us."

"Very wise, Timion."

"Perhaps, Steeleye. But there is more."

Tousle spoke. "This Trok evidently left behind him one of his band after departure, for we detected a weight differential in the lift thrust of the launch, but in the course of our search we did not imagine that the remaining Sylvan would wish to take note of Chaos." His concerned brow deepened. "We were given no advance warning that the Sylvan in question carried a portable teleporter, and before the launch had moved far beyond the Zrost atmosphere, Chaos and the intruder were disrupted on to it. We could not then do anything but protest to the diminishing Trok ship. There would have been little to gain from blasting a launch carrying one of our most valuable creations."

"Please show me the directional beam recordings. I need to get some idea of their distance and movement."

"Come. What news have you for us?" Timion enquired.

"I have a method by which we may achieve our entry into the Sylvan Empire on rather a higher level than you had intended."

"Beware, Steeleye, there are rumours of a greater power than the Sylvas themselves," warned Tousle.

"The Circle of Freefall."

"There is a Circle then?"

"Certainly. Perhaps not as omniscient as one might expect."

"You mean the Circle let you go?" asked Timion incredulously.

"Yes."

"I would not count that as stupidity. There may be sense in apparent madness."

"The Circle imagines that I am going to bring Zrost into its vista of power so that it can compute your histrological potential in what it termed an experiment."

"What experiment?"

"I did not gather that much, but I intend to lead the Circle into believing I am doing as it wishes."

"And you imagine that you can outwit a power that has control over the Sylvan Empire?"

"The more power it has, the more it requires. I can lose little by trying."

"Other than your life."

"I have told the Circle that if I die you will build another and another and another."

"Unlikely."

"There is no reason for it to know that."

"I fear you underestimate this Circle, Steeleye. I think you should beware."

"I shall. Now, we must find Chaos."

Timion led the way into the city tracking building and Steeleye looked at the walls, made from solid Barrier steel, and touched them, feeling relieved that they did not shift and change. Inside, they entered the main chamber which was filled with brightly lit controls, each one carrying equipment that could track a body as small as a pinhead across a million light years into unknown sectors and across all parts of the Sylvan Empire.

The method was called the "Actmum Dust Path" and found its origin, like so many other scientific features in the Universe, with the Eumigs. The system itself was gloriously simple, combining accuracy with complete flexibility. The whole of space and much of matter is surrounded and engulfed by dust particles that float without much regularity, controlled only by the various gravitational forces exerted by matter. The Eumigs discovered that it is possible to use these dust particles as a kind of stepping-stone system across the vacuum of space by firing a charge of Actmum electrons into nil space, or the space immediately in front of the Actmum device. This could then be directionalised wherever required and over whatever distance, and the jump made by the electron could be controlled over large distances. The only requirement was the dust. So long as there was dust, then there was contact in any part of the Universe. The Eumigs had set up vast Actmum generators that swept the skies around the planet over prescribed distances, taking sector after sector of space and analysing the reception value within that space. Every Eumig, or in this case product of the Eumigs, carried a receiver on its person which would react to the Actmum waves and return the signal along the dust path. The waves travelled at several times the speed of light, and distances had to be pretty considerable to daunt the machine. The only problems arose when severe dust storms interrupted the flow of waves, but even then the result was only slightly slowed.

The Actmum Dust Path was a permanent feature of life at this time, and for many thousands of centuries to come, carrying on as the main source of communication right up until the discovery of No-Speed Drive. But that is another story.

Chaos carried a tiny Actmum receiver in her brain, and as she travelled across space in the launch arms of Trok and his Sylvan guards, Steeleye could watch the rapid, weaving path.

"Why does he take so devious a course?"

"The ways of a frightened fugitive, Steeleye."

"But he must know he can be followed."

"Yes, and you had better follow soon, I think," advised Timion.

"It would be better if I went to his destination, and waited for him there."

"Agreed, and we have some ideas on that, too."

"Tell me."

Within minutes Steeleye entered the long-distance teleporter, bound for a planet about which he had heard much from the Eumigs. The planet of Zrost sat at the edge of the Andromeda galaxy, as named by Man many thousands of years earlier, and Steeleye was to travel some 2,300,000 light years across space to a world that Man had also named thousands of years earlier, Earth. For it was to Earth that Trok was bound.

"Remember, Steeleye, Earth is full of snags. It was, after all, inhabited by Man for thousands of years, and no planet can resist impressions for that long."

"You forget, Timion. I am a Man."

71

"You are Steeleye, there is no other, I hope."
Steeleye vanished.

One thousand seven hundred years had passed since Man disappeared from Earth. Almost twenty centuries had rushed by since Man had lived on the small planet sitting alone for the most part in the galaxy of the Milky Way. He had made the best use of his planet and filled it to bursting with his great ambition and power, only to leave it for greater pastures on Zrost. The planet of Earth had undergone a complete reversion during those years from a highly mechanised series of vast cities spread across the whole small planet to a new and extraordinary contrast of rich, plentiful life: huge plains scattered with trees and foliage, small new and strange animal life, and rocky, hilly pastures, quite untouched, undisturbed. It would all seem to the eye as though the cycle of nature had finally begun to open its arms again, ready for a new set of intelligent life. It would seem so, but for strange anomalous features: odd, isolated buildings and manufactured structures which stood out here and there like the thorns of memory in the side of the past. Scattered across the surface of the planet stood whole cities that had once harboured pulsing, energetic life, Man's life. Huge domes welled up like red sores puckered up evilly from the earth, blasted from the rock like boils, blurting out the defiance of history just to remind the humid and wealthy natural life that it could never forget what had been until all was engulfed. The contrast then was as strange as only a living, deserted world could be. Great and beautiful plains of rich, thriving life scattered in the most disorganised fashion with battered, broken and thoroughly dismembered Man-made structures.

The latter-day history of Man had joined and rejoined the major cities so that there were no recognisable centres left, only disjointed parts. On the old continent of Europe, the original capital of Earth was now submerged by forests, humid semi-tropical forests, for the climatic regions had shifted over the centuries.

Steeleye arrived at the point mapped to be the most likely landing place for Trok's launch. The Eumigs knew the Sylvan temperament. They knew that a creature totally accustomed to city life would make for the largest surviving built-up area, which lay squarely central to the direction from which Trok travelled in his evasive manner from Andromeda and Zrost. The place had no name, but had once been called Paris. Little remained to distinguish from it the legends in the annals of the libraries of Afractua. The once rambling and romantic city that housed the contrasts of wealth and indiscreet poverty. None of the boulevardes, none of the corner cafés, nothing of the Seine remained. Only battered, deceived, smooth-edged buildings rambled across an area of three or four square kilometres, surrounded like a comforting muffler with foliage and bush. The forest edge stopped at random points around the city squares and disjointed arcades. Some of the most ancient buildings still stood wrapped in the gloom of a fallen age.

Soon enough most of these ruins would be degraded too. The life of a new nature would eventually overcome the death of the old world. In a slow tide of inexorable lushness, the trees and hedges, the grasses and plants advanced against little resistance, embracing everything in their path.

Steeleye re-emerged at the centre of a complex of buildings, around the place once perhaps the walkway of lovers and prostitutes, the harbour of open theatres. Now all that was left bore reference only to death and decay. The broken structures stood leaning and buckled, smitten by time into softness that crumbles so quickly.

Steeleye walked, looking upon the origins of his parent race, a race of which he had never been a member but of whom he knew much. He wished for a few moments as he stood watching the clouded, slightly red-hued sky that he could take time to travel back and observe Man as he had been then, in his heyday on Earth. Had he been alive then he could perhaps have led Man to a better end than a sour death at the hands of the Sylvans. But now he would seek a small revenge for that death. He would show those cold-hearted creatures how to run an Empire.

The streets were heavily infested with small crawling forms of life, strange unknown insects scurrying across and back from one side to the other, stopping at Steeleye's feet, seemingly regarding him for a moment and then rushing away, without manifest rhyme or reason. Steeleye instinctively avoided stepping on them, and they avoided him as though their bodily memories had still the message of the past trampling feet of Man. The planet life crept out from under the stone and masonry, wrapped around machines, proving nature's strength and consistency yet again. Steeleye stood still. Like a giant among dwarfs, his feet rooted to the ground, his hands on hips, his head regarding the flurry of activity below him. He looked up and saw a flash of light in the near sky. A craft. Trok's craft about to land.

A single bound took him to the nearest building. Trok would not be looking for human life in this long unchartered world. Trok would not expect to be anticipated by anyone or anything, but he would be cautious.

Steeleye surrounded his body with a camouflage of force that would discourage any search beams and sat calmly on a wall by the side of the road, tucked neatly and invisibly away, waiting for his unsuspecting quarry. Only Chaos knew that Steeleye would be there, only she knew, and that by simple human instinct.

The launch disintegrated a million insects as it flashed to the ground, flattened a mass of foliage as it grasped the earth and sank its teeth. Its length measured some hundred metres, its girth tumbled a building, and its weight hollowed out a nest in the ground.

Trok stepped down, sniffing the air and peering through a portable search beam for any signs of aggression. Satisfied that the area was clear he walked round one end of the great launch. So strange to see it in this narrow street. A launch that had measured a dot in space now looked bigger than anything imaginable, squat, cumbersome.

"OK, get her out."

Chaos was carried from the launch by a battle robot and deposited a little roughly on the ground at Trok's feet. She struggled to stand. Steeleye watched. He looked at her body. Her shape had changed. She was rounded, her breasts large and full blown, her abdomen grown to four or five times its original size, her curves somehow suggesting the affluence of additional life, her face bright and more eager than ever before, hair shining, every feature shadowing the people around her. She was pregnant, ready soon to give birth, and in a wilderness far from suited to such a process. Steeleye would have to move fast to release her, get her back to the capable hands of his fathers, the Eumigs. There was little time.

The battle robots scanned the area continuously, and three more Sylvans stepped down from the craft. There would be at least another half dozen inside and the launch had weapons capable of blowing the very earth out from under their feet. A confrontation was not advisable. Craft and cunning were the weapons Steeleye must use.

The area was not ideal—too many little alleyways and doors, not enough open space. But that could also be to Steeleye's advantage. But first Chaos had to be taken away, hidden from danger in some peaceful place where she could give birth to the precious child if her time came.

Almost as though she had received a message from Steeleye, Chaos began to moan with pain.

"What is it?" asked Trok sharply.

"I . . . I think I might be going to . . . have my . . . baby."

"Oh space and cursed Sylvas, not now, not here! Can't you control yourself?"

"How? You tell me and I'll do it. How can I stop a birth here and now in this life foresaken hole. Get me out of the sun."

Trok issued swift orders. "Carry her to a building, and make sure she's well sheltered. And gently, you lumbering great cretin."

The robot was gentle. It carried her to the building where Steeleye waited and laid her down on a moss bed. She allowed a couple more moans to escape from her lips as the robot cooled the area with its hand beam. Then it stood at the entrance with its back to her, and Steeleye, clearly reasoning that a single, helpless, pregnant Woman could show little resistance.

Steeleye was familiar with the exact make-up of a Sylvan battle robot. He had studied the subject with much application, and knew that the drive and motor units for the creature lay neatly at the back of the neck. He also knew that this area of the robotic skin was heavily protected to ensure the longest possible mobility. Sometimes Sylvan battle robots went on fighting and killing after massive damage to the body regions, and even having lost a large portion of the head section could continue to buffet and squash a hundred opponents. He knew that a single, hair-thin shaft trailed through the head section from the front to the back and communicated the orders to the drive mechanism from the brain section in the chest. Hence an order from the chest followed by the severing of that thin shaft would lead to a continuation of the last orders' effects until the robot was stopped in its tracks. Steeleye made his plan.

Outside, the merry band of Sylvans stood while Trok detailed each to his watchpost during the confinement of Chaos on Earth. This could not take too long; there was only a while before all the Sylvans would split up and make the task ten times more difficult. Steeleye looked. He aimed the deadly eye at the roof of the building directly above the battle robot's head and burnt a neat hole, contracting the steel pupil to its smallest, needle-thin aperture. A tiny stone dropped on to the top of the robot's head, the robot looked up, tilting back its head and exposing the one spot where the communications shaft was vulnerable. His aim had to be perfect, and his mind well controlled. He sent out a strong sensory order, instructing the robot to attack, firing its aggressive senses as strongly as he could. He knew that for a split second when the creature was caught unawares by the falling stone its shields would come down from the mind and it would be susceptible to insinuation. Having implanted the order in the aggression centres of the robot, Steeleye, his eye still at the vital spot, performed a perfect lobotomy, severing with one shaft of heat the tiny membrane, thus disconnecting the communication relay to the motor system in the neck. The last order to the robot was to attack, at random and without reference to enemy, straight ahead. The robot thundered out into the open with its six disrupters blasting before it, firing laser and atomic blast weapons at anything and every-thing in sight. The first four disruptor blasts took the entire nose off the launch, the fifth cut down three Sylvans; the sixth totally disintegrated the pilot section of the launch with three Sylvans inside it. A laser beam carved the arm from another Sylvan guard, leaving him astonished and bewildered, falling to the ground only to be trampled to death by the advancing machine.

Trok reacted in style, rolled to the ground and disap-peared under what was left of the launch, racing for cover on the other side. The last remaining Sylvan escaped too, unhurt. The robot stopped for a second and then turned, facing back towards the building from where it had come. It reset the weaponry and took the side off the door from the building in which Steeleye and Chaos watched. But Steeleye was ready. With the sweep of his eye he burned the robot's weaponry free on one side, and severed most of the blaster attachments. But still the creature kept coming. One disruptor continued to function. Steeleye stepped smartly to Chaos' side and swept her neatly up, cradling her soft body in his arms. With two strides he carried her to another part of the building and slipped out through the window.

Now at one side of the robot, he sent a single rapid fire of short, sharp, potent shots, twenty-five millimetres apart, down the very seams of the robot. The creature turned to face him and Steeleye dodged the disruptor fire. He knew he had to knock out that weapon. It took only a scratch hit and an arm or leg could be gone.

Expanding his pupil to full aperture he sent the heat of its strength at the robot, busting the creature wide open and burning up another large portion of the launch behind it. There was nothing left now, but the Sylvan guard was still about. Steeleye detected him, felt his presence and looked to see a small quivering creature, body-changing at a rate of knots beside the launch wreck. The Sylvan levelled a laser at Steeleye. It was whipped from his hand with a blink and the guard fell to his knees.

"Where is Trok?" demanded Steeleye.

"We did not expect you."

"No. Where is Trok?"

"I don't know."

Steeleye picked the Sylvan up with one hand and hung him a metre above the ground, dangling, twisting in indignation and fear.

"Where is Trok? Or would you rather get hot?" Steeleye allowed his eye to boil a little, the Sylvan turning his head violently to avoid the intense heat.

"I tell you I don't know. He ran off into the buildings, he's gone."

"Here I am, Steeleye."

Clever. Just like Trok, defiant at all times. Very clever. Take an adversary much stronger than himself and surprise him, from behind. Steeleye felt a searing heat at his back. The heat of a laser. With the flick of a giant arm, Steeleye tossed the wavering Sylvan into the air, aiming the trajectory towards the beam behind him. The Sylvan fell, but Trok was quick. Quick enough to avoid the crashing body, but not quick enough to stand aside from a small rock that seconds before had been hurled from Chaos' hand, true aim and fast, bouncing nicely on the forehead of the Security leader and sending him reeling in pain. But Trok was a seasoned warrior. Long accustomed to overcoming pain, he used the fall precipitated by it to roll away from the menacing eye. As he went he slipped a three-cornered blade from his belt and let it fly.

Chaos watched the deadly primitive weapon, always carried by the older Sylvan guards, slide through the air as if it moved in slow motion. But its speed was not slow. Its movement was not constant, for like all Sylvan weapons it had an unexpected feature. The molecular structure was controllable. Its shape changed in flight. Like a spinning ball it slipped away and back again, changing size, appearing to be further from its mark than fact dictated. Think of a projectile thrust through the air at you. You watch it from its distance as it grows larger and larger until at its largest it hits you. Imagine that reversed and reversed again. The three-cornered blade started small and grew smaller, as if thrown from a distance in the opposite direction, but coming towards you—like a boomerang moving away only to return, but without the distance of circular travel. Suddenly it grew larger, and then receded again, all within the space of a few seconds. The blade caught Steeleye a blow on the shoulder, slashing his skin and sending gushes of rich blood to the ground. This had to end. Steeleye leapt at Trok. Two strides and he was beside the Sylvan. Trok knew that strength for strength there was no chance of victory. He pressed a button on his belt and sent a force shield around his body, rolled away, buffeted along the ground on the cushion of the field and teleported from the planet surface to who knows where?

There was no time now for wavering. Trok would be back. Steeleye went to Chaos, who lay in the building.

"We must go."

"I cannot, I cannot," she gasped with pain, twisting on the ground, her rounded pelvis contracting with the beginnings of labour. She was to give birth to the child.

"Are you ready for birth?"

"Yes, I have to be, he will not wait longer. You must help, find clothes, water, some warm liquid. Go – I will be all right, but do not be long, for he is your child too."

Steeleye dashed from her side to the burnt-out launch, rummaged in the hull and found water. He took a guard's helmet from a battered body and cupped as much as he could into it. He turned his eye onto the base of the helmet and heated the water. "Here." Steeleye handed Chaos the cloth taken from the arm of his bloodied smock and placed the bowl of water at her feet.

"Help me. Hold my hand, Steeleye, he comes quickly, more quickly."

Chaos gasped, breathed fast, edging the child through the process of pain and pleasure. The small body, creased and bloody, slipped head first, eyes tight shut, gasping for air, from the body of the woman.

The whole birth took only minutes. Chaos cradled the separate body in her arms, wrapped in the thick cloth, and mopped its brow, furrowed and disturbed from crying. Full of fury and anger at being wakened from a beautiful sleep the Man-child fought, arms waving and lungs shouting. How dared they brush aside his wishes and allow him to be born into the crashing mess of a dead world. This was not the place for Steeleye's son and Chaos's child to be given birth. But his mother released her full, milk-flowing breast from the tunic and the child took the large ripe nipple in its mouth, sucking noisily, lapping up the very juice of nature, lavish long pulls, rewarding, fulfilling.

"Isn't he beautiful?"

"He is beautiful, there is no doubt of that. You are some Woman, my Woman Chaos."

"Does Steeleye love?"

"Indeed, yes, Steeleye loves." He smiled, laughed, threw his arm into the air. "Come, Trok, who cares, you will not damage this."

And the Earth night settled over Paris.

PART II

Before

Some thought Steeleye to be no more than a bug on the back of the Empire, buzzing round a giant, nipping at the irritated enemy, soon to be knocked to the ground, crushed under foot. Few imagined that he would prove a constant adversary.

But as the twin suns continued on their journey towards the Complex the Sylvans' own suns were overshadowed, the power set against the Man redoubled only to discover that this persistent fly was not to be crushed by even the most virulent swatters.

Steeleye was here to stay, the LULL was at an end and the storm in sight.

Haephranis, *Biographies of Steeleye*, Universal Annals ref. hgty/5478/76.

Chapter 6

"He's born!" Tousle rushed into Timion's laboratories with the news just received from Steeleye across millions of miles.

"On Earth?"

"Yes, on Earth."

"Apt."

"And exciting, perhaps."

"Are you excited, Tousle?"

"Of course! Aren't you?"

"I'm afraid my synthesiser tells me to be apprehensive, but there is a hint of some other more extravagant emotions somewhere there."

"I have begun preparations to collect them and welcome them home."

"I will come and watch."

The two great Eumigs went to the central city complex where robots moved smoothly with the occasional hop and skip about the streets. The news had been passed around the planet, and a specially appointed group of Eumigs was preparing the festivities for the arrival of the parents and the child so eagerly planned and awaited.

"I wish he could have been born here, it would have been a lot safer."

"No home-coming, though; we couldn't have put up all these decorations, could we?"

"I don't think I can recall a time when we did anything quite like this before, Tousle. But then we have never given birth to a Man-child, so I suppose it is appropriate."

The whole city centre was bedecked with "Welcome"

signs; slogans emblazoning the words "Welcome home Man-child, son of Steeleye!", "Well done Chaos, welcome home" and similar sentiments. The Eumigs were like overjoyed children at a party, bounding about the streets, chatting to one another as though they had given birth themselves.

"How are we getting them back, Tousle?"

"Space launch, Timion, the safest way."

"The longest, too."

"We are taking a complete battle fleet through teleport to Earth and we shall return by space light flight. The journey will take some five days, with a little time-jumping thrown in."

"Why not risk teleport on the return journey?"

"A twelve per cent chance of failure is too great a risk."

"You could lose them anyway. You are giving the Sylvans five days in which to wipe out the whole fleet."

"Since when has a Sylvan fleet dared to attack Eumigs?"

"They want that child," warned Timion, "and they want Steeleye. They won't hesitate this time. Be ready for them, Tousle. We don't want to lose them again."

"I have made elaborate preparations," Tousle reassured Timion. "They won't get near the family, not within a hundred kilometres."

"Tell me about it."

"We are taking fifteen battle launches with full armament, and aboard each launch there is a chamber to be installed for Chaos and the child which will teleport to any other launch in a split second upon attack. The short distance between the launches carrying or receiving reduces the risk percentage to around two per cent, much better odds. The device is automatic and responds to any attack on the carrying vessel. It summons the nearest vessel and the chamber is transferred immediately. This will occur as many times as there are

86

launches and the whole fleet would have to be wiped out before the Woman and child could be damaged by so much as a single singed hair. They won't even know it's happening."

"Very ingenious, Tousle. Congratulations. What about defence and attack?"

"All the launches are fitted with the usual battlement features: long-range disruptors, lasers, cathatars and blasters. We are also taking thirty battle robots, who will travel independently outside the craft but be in constant TI communication with the nearest vessels to them. All the orders are organised through the 'brain traffic communications' from yourself and across all robots. We have also made arrangements for a spin attack if necessary. The order mechanism is already briefed."

"I hope we shall not need it," sighed Timion.

"It is a final device."

"How many Eumigs?"

"Altogether there will be a crew of four hundred, aboard thirty launches."

"And facilities for the mother and child?"

"Nappies, force clothes, centrally heated chamber, liquid and food refreshment, water, extra coverings, first-aid equipment, excretory chambers, medicine bowls, bandages, blood congealers, pins, pyjamas, night gown, ear mufflers, tissue paper, egg timer, emergency heating controls just for the carrying chamber, independent teleport belts . . ."

"Enough, Tousle, enough. You will need a launch just for the accessories."

"Indeed not, everything is packed in reduced molecular chambers."

"You have indeed thought of everything. My congratulations yet again."

"Thank you, Timion. I intend that the precious pair should be comfortable during the journey."

"When do we depart?"

"In three hours. Will you take the lead helm?"

"Of course. I don't intend to miss this trip."

The battle fleet stood ready on the launch pads, all lined precisely in formation. The row of thirty launches, nose forward, stood in exact readiness, their crews standing to attention. The battle robots before them towered in all their magnificent adorned strength, each one on best behaviour. Not a button was out of place, not a precision control belt unshined and ready for action, not a Eumig tired or de-circuited.

Tousle paced the line of power before him, head slightly bent down and great hands folded behind him, back and forth, awaiting the leader's arrival.

Timion inspected the array and boarded the lead launch. Take off was immediate.

Steeleye stood on Earth, waiting.

"Will they be long?" Chaos and the child lay in the cradle of warmth set up from hand blasters at low heat and nestled into a carrier force field, cocooned by science.

"I think not. They are as eager to get you both home as I am, no doubt they are prepared. I expect Tousle is fussing around like a mother himself, for he feels much responsibility for you."

"And you, Steeleye?"

"Yes, I feel more than I ever knew possible. These are new emotions, born out of experience, not from Hamgar's education."

"What became of Hamgar?"

"He is in the Eumig circuitry hospital. They are performing Android restitution on his poor battered body. I think you could say he is recovering from a nervous breakdown."

"Poor Hamgar."

"I thank him, he has given me much to be pleased about."

"Pleased with yourself for producing a child, eh? Typical Man reaction, I should imagine."

They smiled, and as they looked upon the Man-child a small whisk of light raced through the air and Timion's lead launch landed a few yards away without disruption to the surrounding atmosphere. Timion stepped from the exit formed from the seamless surface of the craft and smiled at the threesome on the ground.

"You are safe, thank providence."

"I hope providence stays with us. We have needed it thus far."

"I take it Trok has gone," Timion said.

"I wouldn't be too sure of that. He is a wily old warrior, doesn't give up too easily."

"We are prepared," asserted Timion.

"I will travel with you. I doubt that my feeble strength will match up to a Eumig battle fleet, but I have the advantage of size and speed."

"We would welcome you, Steeleye, if you do not mind travelling alone through space. You must be tired."

"Not too tired to want to make sure of the safe delivery of these two." Steeleye indicated his wife and child.

"Come then, board the launch."

Timion ordered two Eumigs to carry the mother and child to their chamber, which they did without harm or discomfort, lifting up the light burdens with gentle strength.

They set off to lead the battle fleet back to Zrost, but the inevitable tormentor Trok was at hand. He did not like defeat and he knew the wrath of his leaders. He would have Chaos and the child back with him, or die.

The battle that followed was to go down in the annals of the Universe as one of the greatest and most devastating of its kind. There had never been open warfare between the Sylvans and the Eumigs, and no two more powerful races existed in that great Universe. It started modestly, with only a fraction of the available resources on each side, but it grew as the determination grew to win. Later known as the Battle of Earth, it was fought around the planet at much cost to both sides.

"Like two great wrestlers," Tousle recorded after the fight, "the opposing forces of Sylvans and Eumigs addressed one another across space, dancing back and forth through the dead air, weaving and turning, summing up each other's strength before moving in." The Sylvans quickly split into their accustomed defensive array, surrounding their lead launches with a circle of protection, giving the commanders time to plan tactics. Two launches floated in the centre, while ten others moved in an orbit about them, circled again by forty more launches and flanked by the balance. The Sylvans always planned carefully, never rushed in. They would observe a strange propriety, force it upon their opponents, showing their teeth slowly, setting up the code of behaviour, because they knew they could, because they were confident and used to victory.

But the Eumigs were not small; they lacked the cautious approach to battle. The Eumigs stood by, observing the tactical build-up calculated, in vain, to make them apprehensive. The Eumigs placed their craft in a perfect formation, quite still in space, like hostile hovering insects, malicious hornets, their strength quite assured, the end in sight already. And silent. No internal communication, no buzz of orders. The orders were given, learnt and well-rehearsed through all Eumigs, for they knew the mind of their leader.

Thus, while the talk channels of the Sylvans were alive with carefully scrambled and confused snippets of information, deliberately sent out for the ears of their opponents, all was quite still on the other side.

"I grow tired of this," muttered Steeleye across the Eumig launches as he watched the silly meanderings of the Sylvans.

He drifted in space, almost pacing the carpet of vacuum around him, waiting for the action to commence.

"What are they doing?"

"Dallying with us, Steeleye," remarked Timion. "Bear with them, it is a game they love to play."

"I cannot stay here waiting for them to get started." He sent a searing blast of heat from his eye at the nearest circling launch and drilled a neat four-metre round hole through it side. The launch disengaged itself from the *tour de force* and dashed for cover to repair the damage, but the others remained on their continuous turn round the inner launches.

"This is like being at a fun fair. Shall I have another go? I could knock them all out with a dozen blinks."

"There cannot be any harm in raising their temper, Steeleye. They doubt us, and you in particular. They don't know our strength and they plan to upset our calm by their prolonged deliberations. Play the game you wish, have some fun!"

Steeleye took the word as good and with the speed of light flashed across the gap between his group and the enemy, darting like an intoxicated fly through the ranks, sending stings from his sharp eye into the bowels of each launch in range. He damaged eight craft in a single foray, one of them wrecked beyond repair.

The Sylvans grew angry and evidently abandoned their secretive discussions for the more positive aspects of attack.

Steeleye was almost caught in an onrush of fury directed primarily at him.

Six launches turned on him; weaving, sprightly, quick and furious they shot blasts and disrupter fire into the regions of space he occupied. Each one was close, but close to Steeleye could be a millionth of a second after his presence and not be quick enough. He continued to dart with incredible dexterity in and out of the ranks, watching every craft not hidden by another; then he swept away behind them all, coaxing them to turn their flanks to the main enemy.

But the Sylvans were not enraged to the point of stupidity, and they abandoned the small fly for the greater prize.

"Timion dropped the Eumig launches thirty metres through space, in one manoeuvre, avoiding the buckshot approach adopted by the Sylvans," Tousle noted. "Down a further ten metres and then immediately rose through fifty."

The entire Eumig force performed a strange dance, each one following the random rhythms without hesitation. The various attempts to fire at them failed. The first defensive manoeuvre added to the frustration of the Sylvans.

"Sequence attack." Timion's next phase began and Steeleye stood still in space, in complete wonderment. He was superfluous, with the masters of battle doing their devastating work. "Sections one, three, eight and nine, curtail operations, attack in sequence."

The first four craft streaked into action, hiving off from the main formation and grabbing at the Sylvan craft in a perfectly executed movement. It seemed random, but was carefully monitored. One launch swept across the top of the Sylvan forces and nipped at three of them, sending out blasts to carve a portion from each of six of the enemy; the second dashed underneath the whole formation and sent a series of quick, cracking cathatar shots into the pilot sections of three launches; the third, firing at full force, blasted into the centre of the gathering, using a wide-angle shot which superheated ten craft and produced an inferno within their hulls that rendered the crew incapable of performing their tasks. The last of the first four came after this one and shot small active bombs into the off balance launches, knocking them from their formation and handing out some nasty bruises.

The Sylvans were bewildered by this highly organised attack; resistance they had never met before. The whole operation of the first sequence of attacks took only a few seconds, but the result was a stinging depletion of the Sylvan forces, and before Trok could regroup the second phase was under way.

"Send out for help, reinforce attack, get another batch of launches here quick, teleport battle cruisers, anything available!" Trok's orders were tinged with panic. Even he quailed before this machine-gun technique, like a frenzied boxer battering at them with such speed that thought was impossible, let alone action.

"Sequence attack. Sections two, four, seven and ten, curtail operations, phase two sequence."

The next four Eumig launches split away from the formation and went into their own specially planned battle dance, this time to even greater effect.

The first two launches moved at space speed, rating mach ten, perfectly aligned alongside each other, their disrupters firing continuously, and a curious flash exploded from each hull, sending out firework displays of light and heat. They were equipped with a high-tension light, mist explosive, which surrounded their advance with what seemed to the enemy like a halo of bright flame. Seen from the defending Sylvan craft they appeared to be expanding by the minute, charging at the centre of the grouping, now in less than perfect order, burning up as they came and enlarging, diverting the eyes from the deadly fire of the disruptors as the shots seared into the bodies of the enemy launches and ripped them asunder. Eight Sylvan launches exploded into their composite atoms and vanished into nothing. Five more caught the edge of the disruptor fire and were disabled. Trok's lead craft came under fire and lost much of its own fire power as one side was blown loose from the hull. He screamed out more orders. "Evasion, side step, three hundred metres east and west." All Sylvan craft swung

93

away from formation and twisted out of range of the still oncoming Eumig attackers.

"Fire to side, ignore light halo!" They had placed their first blasts and the Eumig craft suffered some unpleasant injuries. But the other two in the second sequence Eumig attack were prepared for this move. They came up from below and encountered the new enemy formation. This time there was a new shock. With skills believed unique to the Sylvans in their high capacity for molecular arrangement, they were somewhat surprised to see the Eumigs perform an operation they themselves had planned.

Timion's next order went out. "Sections five, six, eleven and twelve, curtail operations, attack on phase three sequence."

The next four Eumig craft moved in, two of them increasing their size by eight, to become some three kilometres long and almost a full kilometre in width. They then diminished in size suddenly as they approached, then increased again, disturbing the appearance of their coming, making it impossible for the Sylvans to know their distance or their speed. They raced at the pack of Sylvans, now more tightly grouped and firing at them, then darted off-centre and weaved under and over the enemy. The other two went into a semi-spin attack, twirling rapidly as they approached. The spin technique was another Eumig invention unknown to the Sylvans and unpleasant in its consequences. The spin was so rapid that a haze was set up around them, making it difficult to pinpoint their position. As they spun they sent out a catherine wheel of fire attack, shooting blasts at the Sylvans while they attempted to find the other two craft above and below them. Once again the damage was considerable, reducing the frustrated Trok's forces by ten.

"This must stop! Go for the remaining formation. Away from the attackers, move in all craft to rear of oncoming Eumigs. Attack in static formation, full blasters."

The manoeuvre was rapid but unthinking, for the Sylvan leader had not noticed the movements of the Eumig battle robots who had slipped behind them during the foray. Twenty huge, well-equipped battle robots suddenly appeared behind Trok to slap his already red face by knocking out three launches with their fire power. The natural reaction was to turn to the new attackers and attempt to stave off the ghastly heat of their guns. The battle robots moved even more agilely than their master launches, nipping at the craft from all angles. One robot attached itself to the very hull of the largest Sylvan launch and proceeded to slice through the body metal, cutting with a hand laser as it rode attached like a leech to the hull. It burst through into the pilot section before anything could be done to stop it and, standing on the main control deck, handed out blasts of death to those who stood aghast, knocking out the whole crew in the breadth of a second. The launch wilted and the robot took control, causing still more confusion. But help came. And not before time. Trok was down to less than half his original force, and even that was diminishing fast.

Fifty more heavy-duty battle cruisers teleported to the scene, ready for attack. Timion's problem became more acute.

"Reinforcements have arrived, Timion," Tousle informed him.

"I am aware." He issued a string of orders. "Eight cruisers, numbers thirteen to twenty-one, make spin attack at full rate. Remaining carrier craft steadfast, plus two sideliners for redelivery if necessary." Timion kept in the forefront of his mind the image of his precious Chaos and the child.

"Steeleye, I think we could use your help."

"I thought you'd never ask."

Steeleye sped into action, moving at his highest speed

over the top of the new threatening Sylvan battle cruisers. He dropped rapidly down into their centre. They were grouped close and his body slipped into the areas where fire power was least. He used his own special form of attack, cutting neat holes in the sides of the cruisers, choosing to cut free the engine and weaponry control areas. Without blowing the craft to pieces, he managed to knock out of action three heavy-duty cruisers in some three minutes. But Trok had a plan. At last, with the arrival of help, he could think a little.

He had ascertained which launch carried Chaos and the child, and he knew that if he could get them off the launch the battle would have to end. The Eumigs would not risk attack against a craft carrying what they most sought to protect.

He sent out four of his own Sylvan battle robots to batter at the door of the carrying Eumig launch and watched the result. As the robots hammered at the hull, cutting jagged holes, the second, receiving launch moved closer and the transfer of the teleport chamber took place. Trok moved closer. The battle robots attacked the second launch and as they did, Trok slipped his own launch into position between the carrying and receiving launches, put out his tractor beams and accepted the transfer himself.

"Teleport transfer not achieved. Request orders, we have failed to take on the teleport chamber. Emergency." The Eumig launch bleated to Timion the results of a very clever manoeuvre by Trok, who was already disappearing in the distance.

"Curse them! That was Trok, he has Chaos. What now, Timion?"

"We have no choice. Disable the remaining launches, all spin attack on remaining craft, and let's get back to Zrost."

The last of the Eumig launches went into attack and maimed and crippled most of the remaining Sylvan craft.

Steeleye groaned. "Why the hell didn't you do that in the first place?"

"We don't believe in needless destruction. Come, we must consider the next move."

The limping and depleted Sylvans set off for their Complex. Now they knew only too well the power of their enemy.

Anchor saw the return of a satisfied Trok. The kidnapped contents of his launch were taken quietly and calmly to a comfortable home in the city where they were to be looked after by specially trained nurses. There was no wish to harm the new inmates of the Sylvan Complex . . . yet.

Trok appeared before the Sylvas Council.

"Your mission was accomplished Trok, but at heavy cost."

"The cost is small, my Lord. We have what we required."

"Unlike Eumigs, we are unable to manufacture Sylvan lives. Any loss of life is unfortunate, and in that battle six hundred Sylvans were dispensed with in the twist of a Eumig battle spin. You must produce some method of combating that particular robotic trick."

"Yes, sir."

"But good, no doubt, very good. I will take it from here. Your work is complete in this plan."

"Yes, sir." Trok departed the Sylvas's chamber, well-used to the brusque ways of the leading Sylvas.

Chaos sat calmly in the force rest of her confined accommodation. The Man-child slept again—upset by the disturbances, but well built in the way of his father to cope with discomfort. She looked upon his restful face and feared what life would follow in his future years. Into what worlds had she born this child? What sort of life could she expect for him? Should she have allowed herself to give birth at all? Should she have been stronger with the Eumigs and refused to bear a child? But what choice had she? How could anyone who owed her entire existence to the benevolent plans of the gentle giants on Zrost refuse them anything? They would protect her and her child. Steeleye would take her from danger, there was little doubt of that, and in the meantime she could only rest assured and wait for her freedom. But she waited in trepidation. She knew the harsh coldness of the Sylvans. She had been told of their determined ways, of how they crushed what they could not endure, of how they disposed of whatever stepped in their way. Steeleye and the Eumigs were squarely in their path, challenging and fearless, demanding more than would ever be given, demanding power and recognition, and demanding it without reserve or compromise. Something would give; something, somewhere, would have to step down, and it might begin with her, her and her precious child.

A wavering and twisting figure appeared at the doorway. Continuously changing with every word the Sylvan slid through the room with even more than the characteristic amount of molecular change. He spoke to her calmly and without aggression, with only a quiet authority that sent shafts of cold terror running down her spine.

"Chaos is your name." A flat statement. "We are glad that you have come here to sample our hospitality."

"I did not come, I was brought. I do not wish to be here."

"I am told of your strength and personality. That you are not one easily bent to a will." He ignored her words.

Chaos remained silent.

"We shall be happy for you to remain here until our expectations are fulfilled."

"And if they are not?"

"They will be, Chaos, they will be for sure. Steeleye will come. He does not have the benefit of your female reason. He is impetuous and foolhardy, he will come blasting at us with his revolting eye dealing death and destruction, and we will crush him until the very bones of his Man's body are pulp. There seems little doubt of that to me."

"Then you know nothing of Steeleye."

"I know more than many, for I have met him."

"What is your name?"

"I am known as the Sylvas Lord. I command the whole of the Sylvan Empire."

"I am honoured, you must be a very powerful Sylvan. Yet we do not hear much of you."

"You do not hear much of me, Chaos, because I choose to be unknown. My ways are my own."

"They say that those Sylvans who exceed the body-motion of others have more to hide. Indeed, the Eumigs liken the Sylvan body-motion to a beard on a youth, the covering of malignant spots by the manifestation of adulthood."

"Your tongue works like a Woman's, Chaos, but a very superior Woman. You should insinuate your requirements, they will be met. We shall have more to say to one another perhaps in good time. I hope that you will be saved; you may become a credit to a dead race. Stay alive, Chaos, stay alive."

"And what of my son?"

"Your son? He will die, there is no doubt of that, your son will die, but perhaps not yet awhile, not quite yet."

The Sylvas Lord left the chamber and the door slid to.

Chaos did not sleep that night, nor the next. All in all Chaos remained alone in her sophisticated cell for two weeks. No word or contact from Steeleye or the Eumigs. She watched over her child, feeding, caring, loving, all the time wondering what had become of the Man. Her confidence, and indeed that of the Sylvans, waned a little. Chaos began to think that perhaps attempts had been made to rescue her and that Steeleye was now a mess of atoms, that the Eumigs had given up hope, that all was lost for her and her beautiful son. The Sylvans began to imagine that perhaps their well-laid plans were all for nothing. A tension built up within the Complex. As in all worlds the news got around that Steeleye was coming, that soon the people of the planets would witness a massive battle against one Man. A feeling of heroism slowly developed on Sylva, many thinking that this would be better than any sport. The populace bought viewers to observe the skies and watch for the coming of Steeleye so that they might be the first to inform their friends, so that they might record the great event for their children in future years. The battle of Steeleye would happen; it had to happen soon. And as the days passed, so the tension increased. And this was exactly what Steeleye had planned.

Chapter 7

"You are approaching security buoys, you are approaching security buoys, please lower shields for investigation."

Steeleye obeyed, holding his breath, hoping that the preparations for his arrival in Afractua would be complete.

"The libraries of Afractua demand strict security checks before entry. You must, repeat must, observe all search rulings, your craft will be subjected to search beam scrutiny. Your pass should be displayed on the main control screen." All was prepared as required. "What is your requirement, are you here for pleasure or research?"

"Research."

"What section of the libraries do you wish access to?" The voice was fed into the audio controls of the craft and came out very like an old-fashioned sound computer, stilted and featureless.

"Ancient Sylva."

"Are you aware that this section is classified top security?"

"I am."

"Do you possess the relevant passes?"

"I do."

"Display."

Tousle's inventive powers had been stretched to duplicate a set of top security passes and Steeleye still doubted their authenticity, but the security buoys were evidently satisfied.

"You may pass. Your relevant section is planet 6785.

Please follow the directions on the control video screen, you will be monitored until your arrival. Time is yours."

Steeleye allowed the launch to follow the instructions and sat back to watch through the portholes, observing the different coloured planets, each one surrounded by an artificial colour that designated its function.

The libraries of Afractua were the biggest and most comprehensive reference libraries anywhere in the known Universe and here Steeleye hoped to find out a little more about the Circle of Freefall. Activity was constant, many craft rushing to and fro, containing students, groups of schooling young, tourists, engineers repairing the complex Exon computer systems in the libraries and the many travelling traders who supplied the various rest cities throughout the Complex.

There were some three thousand planets within Afractua and all contained reference material about the civilised and uncivilised Universe. With the right passes anyone could visit any part of Afractua and discover the fascinations of the engineering of time travel, the physics of light travel, the make-up of a video-sector, the geography of Tepor, the number of planets and all details of their functions within the Federation, the biology of a TDK, the medicine of Sylvans, how to make a bio-chamber, how to grow lettuce in tropical climates, what is a monkey, how many Sylvans exist in the Federation, etc. . . . knowledge for ever.

Some spent their whole lives in the libraries, perpetual students. There were rest areas, entertainment centres, apartments, hotels, food halls, everything you could need.

Once in, most were at their ease, for in order to preserve an atmosphere of academe the Sylvans kept the obvious Security guards away from the area. There were no arrest chutes and anyone could walk throughout a planet undisturbed by demands for ID discs. This was intentional, but of course it had its benefits to the Sylvans, for Afractua was a testing ground for the latest security methods—the hidden ones.

Steeleye's launch settled comfortably into dock. Immediate service took over. The exit latches were released from the outside and two servers were waiting at the door. Steeleye would be accompanied by one of these servers throughout his stay. The female Sylvan would attend to his every need, *every need* whatever it might be. The closer and more constant the server, the more consistent the watching. "Havoc Carls." Steeleye had taken on a new identity, using his own chosen name, his real name, given to him by the Eumigs. His face was changed by metabolic restructuring, his body slightly smaller, his clothes much less extrovert. A different person—a Sylvan, in fact.

"That is my name."

"May we help you to your reference section, Ancient Sylva I believe."

"Correct."

"Will you require refreshment immediately, sir?"

"No, I would prefer to start work." Steeleye watched the second server retire and the first, a very beautiful female, as all servers were, take him by the arm in a warm, friendly fashion. She was to be his girlfriend to whatever extent he required for the duration of his stay.

"Is this your first visit, Havoc?"

"It is."

"I hope you will come again."

The familiarity might have been irritating to some, but Steeleye felt no discomfort. He could not afford to—the Sylvans loved it. Steeleye looked at her. She was tall, blonde, and seemed not to indulge in an excess of body-motion. Her body was full, with large, firm, almost heavy breasts, unlike most Sylvan females, who seemed to have dispensed with the bosom as a useful feature of their existence. No Sylvan mother had any need to feed a child, nor even to give birth to one, unless she wished to.

But it was pleasant to see a real pair of large breasts. He was tempted to take full advantage of her service facilities, but that would be too dangerous. He contented himself with looking.

"You wish to see more of me, Havoc? I am available to you should you require me."

"I would very much like to, but unfortunately there is much work for me to do."

"There is always time."

"We shall see. Let me complete my work first, and then if we have a free hour or so, perhaps . . ."

"As you wish." She led him to the section marked "Ancient Sylva" and guided him through the long series of plushly equipped booths, each one some ten metres square, filled with comfortable force rests, cushioned flooring, desks, video screens, 4D crystals, everything a hard-working researcher might need. One wall was a light refreshment counter that would produce whatever was required: drink, food, cigarettes, rest films, stimulants, drugs. The server was qualified to massage, make love, perform first, aid, run errands, jump through a hoop.

"Please summon me whenever you require help. I will be outside the booth." She retired.

"Now, let's see about you, Circle of Freefall. Freefall, Circle: I require full available classified material on the Circle of Freefall, its arrival, make-up, duration of existence, powers and all relevant information.

The Exon computer relay installed in the booth clicked away for a few seconds and the information was read off over the audio screen, spiced with visual displays of the narrative. The Sylvans made everything as interesting as possible. A positive film show. "The Circle of Freefall resides at the centre of the Sylvan Complex, on the planet Anchor, in the Circle chamber at the base of the Sylvas building in Sector f, street reference 59th and ABH. Entry to this chamber is reserved to Sylvas only." Pause for breath and pictures.

"The Circle consists of a perfect geometrical circular shape which hangs without visible support above a question control panel. It possesses absolute knowledge of the workings and functions of the Federation of Universal Powers. It can provide information about any part of the Federation at any time and directs much of the normal day-to-day policies of the Sylvan Empire. It is, however, strictly under the rule of the Sylvas and could not function without them." Likely story.

"It has existed in this place for the entire duration of the Sylvan Empire and has contributed much to the development of that Empire, though rumours to the effect that it possesses life are unfounded and based only on inaccurate folklore."

"Stop!" The account halted. "Relate any existing folklore in this respect."

"Folklore is not accurate."

"Nevertheless, relate."

"The best known but probably least accurate fable goes as follows:

> *Many moons from Sylvan Sands*
> *A million light years gone*
> *There lie the dunes of Freefall Lands,*
> *A world apart from us.*
> *Tis said the Circles flourish there,*
> *That Suns, Twin turning, fill the sky,*
> *That power is greater than we share,*
> *Appalling to the eye.*
> *Thencefrom came, before we began*
> *A harbinger of empires great.*
> *His hands they fashioned one Sylvan,*
> *His mind it shaped a round.*
> *A round so pure that all have feared,*
> *The strength that lies within.*
> *Since that day the Empire's grown,*
> *Admonished every sin.*

> *And now we're great, a might race*
> *And who have we to bless?*
> *The lands of Freefall it is said*
> *But when will they reclaim their sphere?*
> *When will they redress?"*

The server entered, carrying a salver with a tall drink upon it.

"I did not order a drink."

"I thought that you deserved a break, Havoc. This is hard work."

"That is thoughtful of you, but I have hardly worked very strenuously."

"Most Sylvans spend less time than you before they require refreshment. May I sit and aid you further? Perhaps a massage?"

Steeleye recognised that this was all part of the surreptitious security on Afractuan planets, and decided it would be best to go along with the server's suggestions. A drink could do little harm and no one knew he was there, so time was not important. "Very well. Please sit and talk to me while I drink."

"That is kind. My work is sometimes a little empty of interest, and very few who come here wish to do anything other than make love to me and work, usually in that order."

"Do you not enjoy making love to Sylvans?"

"Of course I do, that is why I work here."

"Do you have any choice whom you serve?"

"Some. We are allowed to refuse ten Sylvans a day."

"So how many times do you change your master?" Steeleye was genuinely curious, though any snippet of information might come in useful.

"I usually have to serve thirty Sylvans in a day. They do not stay long."

"And you make love to all of them?"

"Sometimes I make love up to twenty times a day."

"You must be very strong."

"I am specially equipped for the task."

Steeleye could hardly help stifling a laugh.

"You find my situation funny?"

"A little . . . well, no, not really. I was not laughing at you, merely at the slight absurdity of the constant demand for sexual encounter in a system devoted to learning."

"There are other things than video tapes, you know." The server wriggled her hips in a well-practised gesture of provocation.

"So it would seem. What have you put in this drink?"

"Semas juice, mixed carefully with Atrafa and lemon essence, a pleasant combination I hope. It's very popular with my clients."

"You evidently encourage the licentious nature of your clients! The balance of Semas juice with the other ingredients makes for a pretty powerful aphrodisiac."

"It is very popular," she reasserted. "Would you like to make love now?"

Steeleye grew cautious; this overemphasis on close contact made him uneasy. Perhaps they had discovered him—it had happened before. "Thank you no, I must continue my work."

It was the worst thing he could have said. Before his refusal, the server had taken him to be a normal Sylvan who perhaps possessed the last remnants of shyness. But now she was suspicious. She left the booth. Steeleye continued with his research, but she returned only a moment later.

"My pardon, Havoc, I will not trouble you again, but I must take the empty tumbler and reset the tape dial."

"What tape dial? I have not finished my drink." He knew that something was wrong, he knew as she passed behind him that she would do something to damage him. He did not know what until he felt her hand brush the back of his neck. So lightly that he almost did not feel, but he knew. There was nothing he could do, he was going under, the powerful drug she had administered was taking effect, he could not fight it.

"Curse you, what do you think this is, who are you to . . ." He fell to the floor, grasping at the table, tumbling everything in sight. Steeleye was big, and as he lost consciousness his body returned to its former and real shape. He grew almost a metre in height, his powerful shoulders expanded to their full width and his entire body crashed to the ground. The server gasped and ran from the booth, soon to be replaced by Trok, who stood triumphant over the captive Man.

"At last, Steeleye, at last I have you!"

"There is more to having me captive, Trok . . . than landing . . . the fish . . ." Steeleye passed out.

"I wonder what you will make of the time dungeons, my friend," gloated Trok. "Take him!"

Chapter 8

No sight, no sound, no smell, no touch, no time—
nothing. If ever there was emptiness, then this was it;
if ever there was total loneliness, then this was worse,
for the time dungeons were the Sylvans' torture, the
place where expendables where thrown, the hole into
which living creatures were cast to rot with insanity. The
place against which death was a dream.

There had always been torture chambers where sight,
sound and smell could be eliminated, but no one before
the Sylvans had ever perfected the art of disposing with
touch and time. There had always been counted sheep,
days and nights, however inaccurate, and touch. Touch
was reassuring, but in the time dungeons touch was gone.
The victim could not even feel the lines or extremities
of his own body.

But as there was nothing, so also there was everything,
for these timeless, dimensionless voids held the mind
of their victim, and from a mind, in a place where past,
present and future are one, there is much to feed upon,
much to see and feel in that mind, before it goes to the
hell of total insanity.

Steeleye's mouth spoke the soundless words . . .

"Hello, I am here, this is me, Havoc Carls, Steeleye,
the great Man, Steeleye the conqueror. Hello! Hello!"
But there was no reply, for no one was there to hear.
Had there been anyone they would have lived only
minutes before dissolving to nothingness, bent to
distraction, broken and bowed before the power of the
Sylvans' retribution. But through his mind there were

images, pictures of himself, his past and his future, his when and his now.

"Look upon me, Steeleye, I am your father. Look on me, for I am Man, Man of your disconnected past, Man whom you have never seen, Man that you were never born to." Floating before him now was a grotesque, transfigured creature that resembled Man in the midst of his final death agonies at the hand of the Sylva. The image floated before Steeleye, twisting and turning in front and behind him, wavering maliciously, swiping at his face.

"Watch me for the last time, for I could have saved you, you could have saved me, had you come before, had you travelled back to me and given me your strength against our enemy. But you did not, you chose to go for your own greed, you chose to break through the conventions of the world and rush in at the Sylvans, tried to win it your own way, just like we did. And now you are lost, now you are broken. For you will not last long in this place, for this is the hell we spoke of in our old religions that you despise now, this is the place of the devil. Suffer it, Steeleye, for death will come, and death will be a blessing."

Steeleye winced, rushed at the image, grasped it with arms that he could not feel, spat with a tongue that could not speak.

"This show of temper will get you nowhere, Havoc, for you cannot fight what is not there."

"Who are you?"

"Who am I? Do you not recognise me? I am your son, I am the child that Chaos has born, and now she will rear me without you."

"Go! Go from me boy, go, I cannot stand to see you."

The young boy knelt before Steeleye, rested his head upon his knee, cried and the tears ran in rivers down Steeleye's legs, the tears of a son he would never know. Yet this was he, without doubt this was the son of

Steeleye. "Don't leave me father, don't leave us both, we need you, Steeleye, we need you, need you . . ."

"Leave me, go back to your time, live your own life, but leave me now, for I will go mad with the sight of you."

"She is waiting, Chaos loves you, wants to see you, we are alone now, we shall be alone always."

"Go . . ." Steeleye's agonised voice seemed to echo, crashing the sound across the Universe, but there was no one there to hear him now, not even his son. Although his presence had been a torment, now that he had departed Steeleye felt the awful knowledge that he would never see his son again, and he was alone, quite alone.

Steeleye floated. His body-mind connection slipped into non-attachment, absolutely featureless, memoryless, all-knowing confusion. He had heard tell of the time dungeons, he had heard tell that no one ever returned from them, that all died from chronic insanity.

He feared this place like nothing he had ever feared, for his powers were seemingly useless to him; strength got him nowhere, his eye was without value. There were no points of reference, no significant reasons, nothing to grasp, nothing to hope for. Why should he bother struggling? Why not give himself up? Why live in hell when you can die in it?

"Ha! Steeleye the magnificent, Steeleye the great! What has become of you now, Steeleye, beaten by the Time Magician, beaten by a lousy Sylvan Lord!" The mocking tones rang out.

"Actual. I wondered when you would come." At first, Steeleye really believed he saw Actual.

"I am the Lord now, Steeleye, you are gone. I am older but still in control. I even rule the great and mighty Eumigs now. Without you, Steeleye, they gave way and we overcame them, reduced them to our rule. We turned them against you, broke them, killed Chaos, killed your puny newborn son. We burnt them, Steeleye, burnt them at the stake like they used to do on Earth thousands of years ago. I thought it appropriate. I knew you would approve; after all, they were *human* were they not? So we gave them a suitably primitive death. Do you approve, Steeleye? Approve, do you approve?" The voice rose to a crescendo of screaming madness, the leering, twisting face of Actual only centimetres from Steeleye, taunting, teasing.

"I don't believe you, it's all a fake. I don't believe you, you're all fake!"

"Very well Steeleye, let me demonstrate, let the Circle send you a movie of the show. They can be acquired easily enough, you can buy them on the local stalls. Lots of Sylvan families have them for home movies, for the entertainment of the masses—the burning of fleshly Woman, and succulent child." And then came pictures of Chaos clinging tightly to the child, both quite naked, being dragged through the streets. The Sylvan guards lashed her, committed the most awful atrocities upon her body, and, eventually snatching the child from her arms, stabbed him many times with Trok's three-cornered knife. Chaos was grasped by three Sylvans, her arms and legs spread wide, her body battered and raped by the lusting Sylvan males in the watching crowd. She was thrown onto the pyre and roped to a stake. Thousands of Sylvans gazed at the spectacle, laughing and jeering. Steeleye could not turn his head in any direction without seeing the ghastly sight.

"There she goes, Steeleye, and there goes the dead child, thrown onto the fire. Say goodbye, say goodbye, for this is their fate, Steeleye, this is their hell. You have your own to contend with."

And Actual was gone, with his magic lantern show.

"Think, think, got to think, got to keep my mind. Sing something, get a rhythm going, got to keep sane. They want me to go mad, so for that reason alone I will not. That wasn't my son, that was an image, not Chaos, just a picture. Actual wouldn't kill her and certainly not in that way – it's all my fearful imagination. No wonder people go mad, I will not, I will not, I will create an image, a series of sounds, but what, what can I hear?" And so Steeleye tried to keep his mind clear and active with as much thought, as many words as possible. He felt like a bubble in the mist of foaming cotton wool, like a speck of atomic microcosm floating amidst clouds of supporting vapour. "What do sleepers do, what do dreamers do?" he wondered in his slowly failing mind. "What do insomniacs do, how do they get to sleep? Rhythm, order, logic. Well, worth a try."

Steeleye found himself tapping. Tapping through the insinuation rhythms of his tiny, brain transmitter system, just simple rhythms, tap tap tap . . . tap tap tap . . . tap tap tap . . . each tap was in perfect rhythm with the next. Then he became more daring, Tappity tap, tappity tap . . . and again still more complex sounds and rhythms, like someone acquiring a new skill.

So it was with Steeleye. At first the rhythms were slow, and then as he began to get more assurance he found a modicum of fun in a nightmare world. He tapped more complex sounds, tighter ticks, flowing more easily. At least his sanity was there.

"What? Something happened. My hands, I felt my hands. Something, life, give me . . ." But it stopped. As he let the concentration go, so also the feeling and sound he had experienced ceased.

"Start again, do it again!" He tapped and tapped, and the feeling returned.

"My hands again, I can feel, I can hear and see." He was drifting, floating in mid air. And breathing, definitely breathing. Time was constant, all the dreadful images were gone. Light became visible. It was the rhythm, it had to be the rhythm. He had imposed order on chaos. He had made a pattern where before there was none. He was shattering the time dungeons. He looked around him. There were no walls, or doors, there were no confines. He floated in the middle of an area of space between the planets. This was a sort of vacuum of dimensions, an emptiness of sensations. The insanity and imprisonment came from self-inflicted stimuli. Because there was an artificially induced void the prisoner allowed himself to sink, drown.

Steeleye intensified the rhythm, turned the volume up full blast and there was a sudden cracking, a sort of gasp, as though the air had gone out of a balloon, and with it Steeleye found himself projected some several hundred metres. He was out, free from the most feared and deadly punishment in the Universe, just like that. Now, from chaos to Chaos, and his beloved child.

Like a massive power force, relying on surprise and his indomitable strength, Steeleye raced to the city centre of Anchor, knowing that she must be there. He burst through the guards, blasting with his eye, to the offices of Actual. With a single thrusting step he rushed the leader of the Universe and wrapped his powerful arms about the Sylvas' waist, trapping him. The whole journey from the edges between the planets where the time dungeons lay to the main administration building looked like the wake of a battle robot in fury; total devastation, Sylvans lay burnt to cinders, vehicles crashed and still, the very ground blasted away as a track from rolling tanks. The door of Actual's office bore the traces of two broken guards splattered against them with the full force of Steeleye's plundering body. Now Actual gasped for air as the giant Man held him in a vice-like grip.

"Where is Chaos? Where is my son?"

"Stop, for the sake of . . . let me go, I can't breathe . . . please, let me go or . . . I will not live to tell . . . you . . ."

Actual, the arch Time Magician, was trapped by simple brute strength.

"You will not escape my wrath this time, Actual. You

have betrayed me all along, and I will kill you now if you do not tell me! Order your guards to bring her and my son here to me. Order them!" Steeleye intensified his grip. Actual let out a cry of agony as his bones cracked, his body giving under the massive force.

"Guards!" he cried. "Bring the Woman and Man-child here . . . quickly . . ."

Steeleye punished the Sylva, never letting go, squeezing harder all the time. "Thought you could dispose of me in one of your silly dungeons did you? Thought that Steeleye would be raped by his own mind, eh? Wrong, weren't you? Surprised?"

"But how . . . no one has ever . . ." stammered Actual.

"I am not just anyone, Actual. When will you get that in your nasty Sylvan head? I am Steeleye, gift of the Eumigs to the Universe. I am not a foolish Man, built only in the image of Man. There is more to me than you have imagined and that is your undoing, Actual, Time Magician, Actual the Sylvas leader, the deceiver, the great body-motion master. Now where is your magic? Now where are your leading orders? All you can do is palpitate like a butterfly in the hands of *your* master. I am your master, Actual. Your leader."

Chaos and the child arrived, but Steeleye did not let go of his prey; gripping with only one arm he released a teleport belt from his waist and wrapped it around Chaos, the child and himself. He released Actual and teleported to Zrost.

PART III

The Storm

Chapter 9

"That's another feature of Sylvan rule you can put a stop to when you take over, Tousle; that was not an experience I would wish upon the worst criminal."

"No one has ever broken the seams of a time dungeon before, Steeleye. You may be sure the Sylvans will find ways of securing it against further attempts. Come, I think you could both do with a rest. A diversion, at least. I think you have never really seen the extent of my brilliance—shall I show you?"

"Please, we would like that." Steeleye and Chaos walked arm in arm, smiling at the leading Eumig before them.

"Have you named your son yet?" Tousle asked as he led them to the centre of his labs.

"We have."

"Boy." Chaos uttered the word smoothly, softly.

"Boy? That is a good name, but one day he will be a Man."

"Well, then we shall call him Man." Steeleye smiled.

"Very good, why should he suffer the same name all through his life."

They entered the force door to the labs and were met by a magnificent array of equipment.

"This, Chaos, is where you were built," Tousle said proudly.

"And tested."

"What was wrong with the tests? Do I detect a note of derision?"

"Of course not, Tousle. It was all very exciting, one is not born with full knowledge every day."

"I would hardly say full knowledge my dear, but a good quotient of it. Steeleye, you have seen all this, perhaps you would like to study that panel and screen over there . . . I think there may be something of interest to you. I will take my young female friend around the gallery of monsters."

Tousle swept a covering "Invisiator" away from the entrance to the next vast chamber. This was what he called his gallery of monsters, and it consisted of all the extinct creatures he had recreated, each one standing in a tall force cover, lining both sides of the walkway.

"This is the gallery of which I have spoken to you, but first I must show you the greatest invention of the Eumigs." He picked up one segment of a large bank of similar segments. The piece was about two centimetres square, heavy and metallic. "This is the Exon. In fact this is three hundred million million million million million exons. Invented by the Eumig Exon, it relies upon the Spot Wave, a memory electron that can exist in any state, that can store information within a chosen body, and Exon chose the micro-proton, one of the smallest existing pieces of matter. Within this small composite each micro-proton carries enormous amounts of information. Within the size of a micro-gauge pinhead it is possible to get a ten-million photon spot cell return on information stored over one hundred years of an injection cycle."

"Not bad, not bad at all," teased Chaos gently.

"Not bad? It's incredible."

"It is, you're right quite incredible."

"The Exon computers in this lab measure three metres across, so that you can imagine what their capacity is. There is plenty of unused space within them, in fact enough to last me the rest of my life."

"Your life? You mean you will die one day?"

"Well, wear down is more the point, but long after you

do. About three quarters of a million years from now, actually."

"Hmm, I wish I could live that long."

"I'm not sure you would like it after half a million years. Life could become a little unlivable to a human over so long a period."

"What can the Exon do?" asked Chaos.

"It can do anything, it can give you the answer to any question you choose to ask it, from the whereabouts of the Fisk flower on Cathandramis to the construction pattern of the TDK."

"That wasn't part of my education. What is a TDK?"

"Ask the Exon," suggested Tousle.

"What, me?"

"Why not?"

"Tell me what to do."

"Come now, you know how to handle an Exon, it was part of your training."

"Very well, Exon, set question."

"Exon working." The machine spoke gently, humanly.

"Simplified definition of the TDK, please."

"The TDK, common term for *Terrandora diclytus kiphthalamus*, found in the higher regions of the mountain range of Gorton, on the planets of Fifth Grid, Warnick and Forn, in the system of Has, Galaxy 456, named Ytam. The *Terrandora diclytus kiphthalamus* suffers the largest known brain area combined with the most inefficient memory capacity in the known Universe. A quadruped, its brain size is approximately eight times that of the Sylvan, and four times that of the Eumig, but its memory capacity is virtually nil. It contains three hearts, each one using eighteen valves, and a bodily drive mechanism of huge proportions.

"Attempts have been made to improve the memory capacity of the TDK, but without success. The most notable scientist in this field is Tousle from the planet Zrost." Tousle blushed.

"It is said of the TDK. 'You'll never forget a TDK, but he will'."

Chaos laughed.

"A pathologically forgetful genius," said Tousle.

"How fascinating. Have you ever seen one alive?"

"Yes, of course, I have worked on them for years."

"Oh yes, the most notable scientist."

"Indeed. Come, let's look at the great gallery."

"What's that?" Chaos exclaimed at the sight of the first strange creature, standing death still on a raised podium.

"That is a Ty, a mammal, seen most prolifically on the planet of Abelitius. It has four legs and stands about a metre from ground to shoulder. In life, it carries a poison sack that ejects a steam-lime substance. It can kill a dozen creatures with one blast, very potent poison."

"And this horrible looking thing? It looks a bit like Man."

"It is similar, it's called a Spanman in fact. A real psychopath, no conscience, no moral laws at all, a complete atheist, very intelligent, but utterly amoral."

"Where do they live?"

"Most of them are in penal colonies around the Federation, or in time dungeons. The Sylvans cannot afford to tolerate them."

"Why not?"

"They hate, or rather fancy, Sylvan females. A Sylvan will kill a Spanman on sight, and not without good reason, for they will rape and murder a Sylvan female as soon as look at her."

"Wow, with that great thing too." Chaos gasped at the huge genitals.

"Yes, they are not unlike the ancient Satyrs, in Earth mythology. They seem to have a strange obsession with the cold-hearted Sylvans, something to do with their unyielding nature."

"There can't be too many of them left."

"Oh, don't think that. They breed at a terrific rate, and if a Spanman mates with another creature, provided that it is vaguely similar in type, there will always be born a Spanman, never a hybrid. The genes are very dominant. And aborting the foetus is very difficult, so that a Sylvan female who gets caught by one will probably have to give birth."

Chaos shuddered. "How horrible."

Tousle continued the tour. "And these are the Tripp and the Fetripp, up there is the Netratripp. Three sexes: male, female and neuter. Note the differences."

"The Netratripp doesn't look very sexy," commented Chaos.

"As you might imagine, it does not reproduce. One in three Fetripp births is a Netratripp, just enough to rule their forgotten world."

"Extinct."

"Yes. They lived on the planet Blue in Faraway, galaxy number 546/d, in the Sylvan register. They survived for something like a million years. The Netratripp ruled all through their evolution, a very shrewd political breed, but Blue suffered such terrible climatic conditions that they continually lost large portions of their population to dreadful earthquakes and storms—it must have been a very nasty world to live in."

"Why didn't they leave?"

"The Tripp race was agrophobic, all of them. Couldn't abide space travel. They would rather die than leave their world, and of course in the end they did."

"And we think we've got problems," commented Chaos.

"Now, this one is the Phtal, perhaps the ugliest creature I know of. You see that thin slit along the middle of the head? That is mouth, eyes, hearing and speech, all in one neat little orifice. They breathe oxygen and convert it into carbon monoxide with the help of the only foodstuff they consume, a bastardised form of petroleum spirit. Nasty, very bad breath they have."

"Where do they live?"

"On the planets of Whey."

"Oh, I've heard of the Phtal of Whey. Weren't they responsible for the Circuit wars?"

Tousle nodded assent. "Then there is the On of Battle, the Casamupo, the Ufutrem, an unpronounceable name for an unpronounceable people from a world with an incomprehensible language. This is the When," he indicated, continuing round the gallery, "that the Shemat he is the Gumcurs, and that is one of the Glass people from Towndown, then the Burners, the Fodors, and here is someone you may know."

"It's Steeleye!"

"Yes, a clone of Steeleye, lifeless at the moment, but I could easily bring him alive."

"That's horrible. How can there be two Steeleyes?"

"You know full well there could be hundreds of Steeleyes now, once the prototype is made I can clone hundreds in no time, but I won't. One is sufficient.

"What if someone got hold of that and brought it alive without you knowing?"

"Then they would have more trouble than they had bargained for. It possesses all the characteristics of the real Steeleye, and anyone trying to juvinate it would suffer the consequences very quickly."

"I still don't like it much."

"There's nothing to fear. In any case only I know the combination for opening the force field around him, and even then my bio-chambers are operable only by me. They need my TI instructions to work at all."

"I hope you're right."

"Was I ever wrong?"

"You didn't build the first Steeleye, that was a mistake."

Tousle said nothing.

"One day, millions of years from now, when you're

gone, the Eumigs are gone and the Federation finished, someone will come here and find your collection. Imagine the surprise, what would they think of this gallery of ghouls?"

"In millions of years, my dear, the people of the Universe will know much more than we do; they will have records of all the animals and creatures here."

"You're so unimaginative."

"Naturally."

They walked back into the main labs to see Steeleye leaning over the screens before him.

"Well, Steeleye, what do you make of that lot?"

"Very exciting. These must be the Twin Suns the Circle was talking about, the great Twin Suns in the legend I dug up in Afractua. The twin Suns of Freefall."

"Correct, and they're heading in this direction, one on either side."

"Either side of what?"

"The Federation." Tousle paced the floor before Steeleye, pointing at the video screen. "And they've been here already."

Steeleye turned to watch the great Eumig. "When?"

"About the time of the beginning of the Sylvan race."

"Just like the legend said."

Chaos sat and listened to them both.

"So you think the Twin Suns actually created the Sylvan Empire, put it there, like . . . like . . ."

"Like a game of chess." They both turned to look at Chaos.

"Yes, just a move in a game of chess. As if they wanted to set up an experiment and watch it move about a Universal board."

"Very poetic, Chaos, and not far from what might be the truth," said Tousle.

"And when do they get here this time?"

"In about a month, a bit less perhaps."

"You mean you haven't computed it exactly?"

"Twenty-seven days, four hours, three minutes and fifty-four seconds, actually."

"I might have guessed."

"And you will have to face them if you are going to put yourself in power."

"That should be fun."

"You'd better get to work, my friend. You cannot afford to waste much time."

Chapter 10

"I want direct contact with a Sylvas, this is urgent." The Director of the Power Source Centres on Crictor, well known for his nerve in dealing with superiors. shouted the instruction over the sub-space radio.

"Hold one moment, your request will be considered."

"I haven't got time for it to be considered. This is an emergency. Put me on to a Sylvas right now or I'll see you in a time dungeon."

"You are through to Timmis . . ., sir."

"My Lord Sylvas . . ."

"Yes, Director? Being rude to my operators again I hear."

"My Lord, I think the power stations are about to go up in smoke." Always to the point.

"What on Sylva do you mean?"

"Just what I say. There is a small package that has been found attached to one of the central power systems and it looks like a substance my chemists tell me is Pactrac."

"What is Pactrac?"

"A natural explosive from Andromeda planets sir, mostly found on Phumus."

"Who goes to Phumus nowadays, those blessed Eumigs have taken it over . . ."

"Exactly, sir, the Eumigs. It could be some kind of trick, but I think it's a little dangerous to rely upon that."

The Sylvas Lord pondered. "Has Steeleye been spotted in this area recently?"

"Certainly, sir, he was laying the contact track for the Circle to Zrost. We gave him full clearance."

"Well get the blessed Pactrac or whatever you call it off the plant."

"Can't, sir. It's got a force seal on it, and if we blast it the whole plant could go up."

"I see." Long pause. Very long pause.

"My Lord?"

"I'll call you back." Timmis cut contact. The line flashed again.

"My Lord Timmis?"

"Yes, Operator?"

"I have a sub-space request from the Director of the School Centres on Phanadal."

"What does he want?"

"He says it is an emergency, and he must speak to a Sylvas."

"Am I the only one in office today?"

"Yes, my Lord."

"Very well, put him on. Yes, Director, what is it?"

"My Lord, we have found a rather disturbing package attached to the main school building. It contains an unknown substance, and we cannot detach it from the school because it seems to be stuck there, sir."

"What you mean, Director, is that it is force sealed, and you cannot remove it by any other means than by blasting it away and taking the building with it."

"Well, my Lord, we could certainly put a blaster to it . . . I hadn't thought of that. Just a minute, I'll get one of my guards on to it. Guard?"

"Director . . ."

"Guard, come here, I want you to . . ." Timmis listened to this conversation with growing horror and alarm. He shouted over the radio frequency.

"Director, will you listen to me . . ."

The Director's voice came over loud and clear. "Get a blaster to that package on the school building, make sure the children are aware that there might be a small bang, nothing to worry about . . ."

"Director! Damn you, listen."

"My Lord? That's done now, the guard will . . ."

"If that guard blasts the package, I will personally sever your head from your body . . ."

"My Lord?"

"Stop him, stop him now" The Sylvas shouted down the receiver at the top of his anguished voice.

With relief he heard the Director again. "Guard, cancel that order, don't blast the package. Stand by and await further orders."

"Good, Director, very good, my congratulations. That package probably contains a substance called Pactrac, which is a natural explosive of very high magnitude, and if you blasted, it could devastate the entire school building and much of the surrounding area. Evacuate all the children to the other side of Phanadal, get them as far away as you can. Got that?"

"Yes my Lord. I apologise, my Lord."

"Good day, Director . . ."

Contact broken. Timmis picked up the internal telephone receiver to call Actual, but his sub-space receiver blurted again.

"Yes, Operator?" he sighed.

"Another call, from Stradt this time, my Lord."

"Very well. Yes. Director?" wearily.

"My Lord, this is the Director of the Exon on Stradt . . ."

"Where's *your* package?"

"My Lord, I have a package . . . oh, you know about it?"

"Where is it,"

"It's attached to the central Flexspots terminals, my Lord, I daren't take it off."

"You cannot take it off, Director. It contains Pactrac, and you would blow the whole communications system in the East 4 sections and we can't have that, can we? So don't touch anything. Understand?"

"Yes, sir, my Lord, sir."

Timmis cut contact, and called Actual.

"Actual, we seem to have an epidemic of Pactrac."

"Explain."

"Three planets, Crictor, Phanadal, Stradt, so far have reported small packages attached by force beam to vital parts of the central systems, including the school, all chock full of Pactrac, which no doubt you know . . ."

"Contains a natural explosive, yes Timmis, I know, and I also know that my three children are in that school right now. There's a special firework display there today, and nearly ten million children will be on Phanadal. Timmis, this is Steeleye's work."

"Yes. What do we do?"

"Get the children away for a start."

"We cannot take them all off the planet at once; it took nearly four hours to get them there. We can only move them away from the school area."

"Then do that, and tell all the Directors to sit tight, there are likely to be more on other planets. Send Trok in, get his Security working, get guards doubled up on all the planets, now. I'll be there in a few moments."

"Yes, Actual." He put the internal telephone down, and turned to the radio receiver to hear the latest messages.

"My Lord Timmis, there are three other sub-space calls for you, one from Afractua, one from Fac, and one from Pinalis, oh, and a fourth from Cris."

"Put them all on audio together, operator," He addressed them collectively. "Gentle Sylvans, please listen to me. I am aware that each of you is calling me with urgent news that there are packages attached to vital pieces of equipment on your planets. Please do nothing. The packages contain Pactrac, which is a natural explosive and will blast the hell out of the equipment if you try to remove them. I repeat, do nothing, leave them alone. Trok will be there in a short time with Sylvan forces to help you, but on no account touch those packages, and take steps for the immediate evacuation of the areas." Timmis cut contact.

Then the fun started. Timmis switched on his multi-screen, attached to the Circle, intending to speak to it and ask advice, but there was much activity already in the Circle centre. Timmis watched the screen light up in his chamber, so also did Actual, and each of the other Sylvas, one screen in each of their dwellings across the planets. Each screen showed a vast explosion, on Crictor. The power plant was devastated. One moment the power plant that supplied almost the entire energy to the Sylvan Complex was there, in all its complicated glory, and the next it was gone, razed to the ground.

"Curse the heavens, we're too late! Curse Steeleye!" muttered Actual.

The next moment the air began to clear. The great billows of smoke and steam began to clear and before their eyes the sequence of events was reversed. The power plant began to rebuild; without help from any visible source the whole area began to raise up. There was no film to run backwards, the pictures came across as they happened, accurate, precise, but incredible.

"What in the name of Anchor is happening?" Actual shouted the words at the Circle.

"There is no information for analysis, I have no information." The Circle sounded disturbed, uncertain of the logic, of any logic.

The power plant continued to re-erect itself, lifting from the devastated ground until finally it was complete again, standing as it had before. Exactly as it had before, except for one feature. Around the circumference stood thousands of Eumigs, ranked ten deep, shoulder to vast shoulder they stood, completely in command. There was no doubt, no escape from the truth: the Eumigs had taken over Crictor and the power plant.

Then the picture changed.

"What is this, Circle, what are you doing to prevent them? "

"There is nothing I can do, there are no precedents, there is no method by which I can judge, nothing . . ."

"This is Actual calling Trok, Trok where are you?"

"I am on my way to Crictor, my Lord."

"What good is it going to Crictor you imbecile? You're too late for that. Go to Phanadal, now, quickly, get as many troops there as you can. Hurry, you idiot."

"Yes, my Lord."

But too late again. The picture came up on their screens, the school blasted to kingdom come and then resurrection. The hellfire and brimstone of the blast was beyond anything Actual had seen for years, and the rebuilding, this strange inexplicable feat of rejuvenation, was quite beyond him. But it was happening again, the whole building growing out of the ground like a malignant fungus in perfect duplication of the smashed steel. Impossible, ridiculous.

The picture switched yet again, across the planet to the play area where all the children had been evacuated. They were all there, millions of them in one great valley enclosure, and about them stood still more thousands of Eumigs, rank upon rank, standing staunch and still about the precious gathering. The firework display was in full swing, great arcs of light flashing through the sky to the delight of the children. As Actual watched along with the other nine Sylvas, all aghast with amazement, a message was spelt out in lights, in the sky. "Your children are safe, Actual, safe in the hands of the gentle Eumigs. You are fortunate, for they do not lack compassion. Under their strength and guidance the Federation will go far."

"Curse you, Steeleye Curse your damned arrogance."

Then the flexspots of Stradt catapulted into space with the blast of Pactrac. Then they too were reborn. The great communications systems blew sky high, knocking out the whole East 4 section of the Federation, an area covering some three thousand planets, knocking out their video, 4D, teleport, telephone and all other forms of communication. The machines regrew, but not the communications. They remained dead.

After that Afractua's Exonic computer petered out, the Security forces' main control buildings on Frac collapsed, the space launch factories on Pinalis were no more except in duplicate and the main Exon control on Cris died, to be reborn dead. Actual collapsed back into his force rest, shaking and quivering with anxiety and rage, for on all those planets stood rank upon rank of Eumigs, guarding some of the most vital composite parts of the Federation of Universal Powers. In total command, and more than just bargainers for complete power. The victors. But they still did not have the Sylvan Complex. They still did not have the centre of power, nor did they have the Circle of Freefall. That would never fall to them, not if he had a say in it.

Unfortunately, he did not.

"My Lord Actual, there is something wrong, outside the sphere, something sighted coming from the north, my Lord, it's an army."

"An army of what?"

"Well . . ."

"Come on, Sylvan, let's have it. An army of what?"

"Of Steeleyes, my Lord."

"What do you mean, that there are hundreds of Steeleyes out in space?" Actual was incredulous.

"Not hundreds, my Lord, thousands, hundreds of thousands."

Actual leapt to his feet, his body-motion almost wavering his shape to a liquid mess.

"Call Trok, get him back here immediately."

Actual went to the main viewer next to his chamber, in the chamber of the Circle itself, and watched the activity

133

in the sky. Sure enough, there was an army approaching, a vast army.

"Close in on that, give me a better view." The scope brought the picture closer.

"How many?"

"Ten thousand."

"Blast them, use the main sphere blasters, blast them out of the sky!"

A series of powerful atomic blasts went out from the surface, but the effect was nil, for the quarry had disappeared.

"Where've they gone?"

"On the other side, my Lord, on the south side of the planet complex."

"Switch the scopes, let me see."

Sure enough, there was another army on the other side of the complex, this time double the first number. Twenty thousand Steeleyes. Exact duplicates, each one with the awful eye leering down upon the planet mirror, twenty thousand times, each one ready for action, advancing at speed through space.

"They've reappeared on the north side, my Lord. Twenty thousand there too. On both sides now, my Lord."

"Fire disrupters at both of them, fire quickly." The disrupter beams shot out into space, but both sets of armies vanished.

"They're, on the west and east sides now, my Lord, forty thousand on each and they've reappeared on the north and south double the number again."

"Damn and blast them! Get those disrupters working, all round, get them, blast them, for the sake of all Sylvans get them." Actual wavered and twisted in his panic, and so did those in the streets. For the sight was visible on all monitors, projected across the whole planet surface, into all private homes, to all the eyes of the Sylvan population in the nine planet complex.

"They're everywhere, my Lord, everywhere. They seem to be multiplying all the time, every time we fire a blast at them they double. There must be almost a million by now."

"It's not possible. Get the Security forces into the streets, calm the people, tell them it's a hoax, a trick, calm them down, by force if necessary, but get everyone off the streets. This is impossible!"

The armies of Steeleye doubled, trebled, quadrupled until Actual finally saw the sense of stopping his fire. Then they changed formation. They moved into a circle around the planet complex, joining in one great circular rank, holding arms, a complete circle around the complex. The one rank became two, the two became four, the four became eight. The ranks then split and twisted to one side so that their number criss-crossed the mirrored surface, blotting out the light of the suns, obscuring the stars, filling in the gaps in an amazing geometrical pattern. Like a series of compass lines around the planets they crossed and crossed again, each rank behind the other, all the time doubling and doubling again. There had to be billions of them, advancing all the time, step by step, in a slow march of sinister glory.

The Sylvans were panic stricken. They knew about Steeleye, they knew of his power as one Man. They knew he could defeat a fleet of guards, twist the head from a battle robot, smash a whole launch to pieces. Now there were more, many more than could be tolerated, millions upon millions of Steeleyes, and the people went mad, rushing through the streets, making any kind of order impossible, smashing their way to get to their launches, in a vain attempt to escape from the inevitable.

"He cannot break through the force fields around the planet, he cannot do that, the people will see him stop, everything will be all right." Actual wrung his hands in despair, for his hope was to be unfulfilled. The army stepped through the force barrier without so much as a word or a halt. Rank by rank, they appeared on the inside of the field, a matter of kilometres from the surface. They blocked out all light, making it impossible to get away from them, each rank coming closer all the time.

Actual sealed the door of the Circle chamber, sealed it shut as a last attempt to save himself from this massed attack. But even that was in vain. A small detonation of Pactrac exploded at the chamber door as Actual stepped back and the steel door fell away, a billow of smoke and dust rushed into the chamber and then slowly cleared to reveal the door rebuilt, standing as it had before, but this time Steeleye stood on the inside of it.

Framed in the massive doorway he stood to his full height, towering over Actual, who wavered and turned before him, beaten and fearful, frightened as he had never been. Steeleye seemed huge, solid, unbeatable, his great muscular arms folded across his massive chest, his robes swirling about his feet, glorious in his victory.

Like a magic knight come to his baronial hall, Steeleye looked down upon his enemy, vanquished and confused.

"Well, Actual, the great Time Magician, see if you can trick your way out of this situation. I am here as your Lord, Actual, you are beaten and there is no escape now."

"What have you done, Steeleye? What have you done to my Empire? What have you done? What have you done?" Actual quivered, unable to form sense into his speech, completely confused, devastated.

"I command you to relinquish the rule of the Federation of Universal Powers to me and the Eumigs who stand guard over your world."

"It is yours, Steeleye, everything is yours."

There was a different voice. "But you will have to face the Twin Suns, Steeleye, for they come." The Circle spoke softly, lethargically.

"I see that they come, Circle of Freefall. We shall meet them, we shall talk. It does not change the power of the Eumigs."

136

"Indeed not. I wish you joy in your new command."
And with that the Circle went dead.

"But tell me Steeleye," spoke Actual. "How did the structures rebuild themselves?"

"In the galaxy of Andromeda there is a substance called Teablood, a rejuvenating substance. It is very simple. You mix it with Pactrac, allow it to explode and thereby raise the temperature from absolute zero to fourteen degrees Celsius in a split second, and the Teablood will do its stuff. The duplicates that you saw will melt. They will simply collapse again into the ground, for they were only ice, Actual, only ice. Regard the door behind me."

And behind them the door dripped amd melted to nothing. Actual turned away, sank into a force seat and remained, quite still, his body-change almost ceased at last, for he had nothing left to hide.

Chapter 11

Like a giant, doused, pin-ball machine, the heavens were
dulled. But for the stars, scattered randomly across the
black, there was no relief to the eternal. Nothing seemed
alive; the cut-off of most of the communication systems
and a large portion of the power source left the Federation
a limping and broken replica of its former glorious self.
The Teablood duplicates were melting now as they
reached ground temperature and slowly dissolved, to
drain away to nothing. The whole chaotic mess was
depressive, sad, beaten.

But the pin-balls were coming. Two colossus flashing
across the skies of a thousand planets on their journey to
the Sylvan Complex. They had entered the Federation
untroubled and presently moved in and out of the worlds,
passing by, avoiding contact, preserving life blood. Without touching so much as the edge of an atmosphere they
came, one from each side of the Federation, one from
each side of the Circle, and gradually reached the centre
point of their long experiment where they stopped, as
suddenly as they had set off.

From Freefall, the Universe of the Twin Suns, to the
centre of Sylva they had taken only months to travel, and
now at the end of their trip they stood before all, still
about the mirrored ball of the Complex, quite without
sound or movement.

They remained thus for some hours. Steeleye and the
Sylvas sat uneasily in the Circle chamber, now in virtual
darkness, waiting. After a time and without warning the
power came on, the lights lit up, communications restarted,
the people wondered. The armies of the Eumigs were

returned to their planet Zrost without so much as a by-your-leave, and the images of Steeleye vanished.

Without further ado the power plant, the school, the communications centres, the library computer, the Security centre, the launch factories, the time travel computer — all were restored to their former state, undamaged, without a mark. As though they had never died, so they lived again, functioning perfectly.

Then a moment of silence. Actual looked calmer, even smiling at Steeleye, until the Suns spoke.

"Many centuries ago we arranged an experiment, here in this sector of the Universe, which was to blossom into a fine and just power, controlled by logical, strong people. We set at their centre a Circle of our own making to give greater flexibility and faster results. We hoped that in this experiment we would see a satisfactory development. In this we were mistaken. The development of the Federation of Universal Powers has not been fine or just, it has been overpowering, repressive. Because our code states that we cannot destroy life having built it, it was our intention to readjust the powers of the Circle onto different levels, at a time convenient to ourselves.

"However, the task has been performed for us, albeit in rather crude fashion and at greater speed, but the result is the same.

"The development of Steeleye and the civilisation of the Eumigs were both chance factors in a time arrangement which we had not foreseen. We have thus learnt, and will take note of the results."

There was a slight pause.

"The instructions are now as follows. The Circle will be removed and the race of the Eumig will inherit the power now in the hands of the Sylvas. The Federation will be permitted to develop along whatever lines it will without our supervision, and Steeleye will come with us."

Steeleye stood, quite still, trying to take in the implications of what had been said. The words spelt a new adventure, a gift, asked for and given, but there was apprehension in his mind. He feared, he doubted the people of Freefall, for he knew nothing of them. They were not only strange to him but also manifestly more powerful than anything he had yet known.

There was no choice in the matter for him. He would have to go. There was little doubt of that. But what of Chaos and Boy? What would become of his family? Would he ever see them again?

As though in answer came the voice again.

"We observe the customs of Man. It will be permissible for the Woman and Man-child to come also with Steeleye. Prepare to depart in twenty-four hours.'

"So, you are to go alone, you three." Tousle spoke, and had it been possible for him to cry, he would have.

"We shall miss our makers," said Steeleye, pressing his great hand on the greater shoulder of the Creature Scientist.

"I think I must introduce some tear ducts into the mechanism of the Eumigs. Just a choice few, you understand, but I feel that it might benefit us to experience the ways of crying."

"You grow more like your fathers each day, Tousle, you grow more like Man himself. I am not sure that is a good thing."

"Man had much from which we may learn. You have taught us, Steeleye, and you, Chaos, a little more of their former ways. We shall go back to Earth and see what more can be found."

"Why the interest?"

"Well, as you say, they were our fathers and we should not wish to disregard our relations, however tenuous the connection. In my case the contact is close. I was the first Eumig to be built after their demise, and Timion was built by the hands of a Man. There is much to be thought on that. In any case, I grow tired of beachcombing

140

in Andromeda; I shall have a closer look at the Solar System now."

"Man spent much of his early years doing just that. He found very little."

"He didn't pay a lot of attention to his own planet, though. That is where the treasures must lie. I shall set up a laboratory there, probably in Paris." he decided.

"Ah, Paris," said Chaos.

"Strange memories."

"Not very pleasant. I wish I could travel back there, in time, and have a look at Man as he was in his best days. Paris must have been fun. I've read about it somewhere – music, gambling clubs and strip shows."

"What on Earth was a strip show?" asked Steeleye.

"You pick up the vernacular, Steeleye. "What on Earth" was a phrase of speech in the days on Earth. A strip show was a show in which attractive women removed their clothing slowly and sensuously in front of little men with raincoats on."

"Why did they wear raincoats?"

"Don't ask me, but they did."

"Hmm, Man was even stranger than I had thought. I think I shall organise a visit to one of these strip shows."

"You will have a long trip from Freefall."

"How do you know? We haven't any idea where it is."

"Oh yes we do," retorted Tousle. "I have been communicating with the Twin Suns. They have told me to call upon them at some stage to report on the success of the Federation under Eumig rule."

"Trust you, you crafty old robot, no one else has managed to talk to them."

"They are not very sociable, they prefer to remain unknown to most of the lower levels of intelligence."

"I see. And you constitute a higher level I suppose."

"Indeed, so it would appear."

"So, come on then, where is Freefall?"

"Freefall is everywhere. Freefall is the rest of the Universe.

It is otherwise known as the Wideways, the Sideways Times. You will start I am told on a world named The Crystal Planet. A place with many secrets, beyond us all. Freefall is for ever. The Universe is for ever. The people of Freefall have discovered the infinite. They have tapped time itself to its utmost, and have occupation of all life and all matter and all space."

"I don't follow."

"Well, you will have to learn, they will teach you. They intend that you should be their first outside student. The first living creature to graduate to the ultimate in knowledge."

"Why? Why should they want a Man for that?"

"Apparently they need you, Steeleye, for some purpose the nature of which they would not reveal. They need you for something they cannot perform themselves."

"The all-powerful fathers of the Universe cannot perform a task that I can?" Steeleye asked incredulously.

"Evidently."

"How fascinating. I cannot wait to see."

"There will be much to see, Steeleye, much to see. They gave me the briefest glimpse of their ways, the smallest peep at Freefall's central complexes."

"And?"

"You will need to keep an open mind. There is no comparison with what you have been taught, of what you have learnt. Everything is different, quite different."

"I see that you wish to keep me in suspense."

"A world away from worlds, a Universe away from Universes, a difference unimaginable to the mind, a place where even I could not digest a millionth of the information within my lifespan without their help."

"So, I will need their help."

"You will get it. Your journey to Freefall will be full and busy, for all of you. You will undergo the education of a lifetime, a new lifetime."

"Come, then."

THE TENTH PLANET

EDMUND COOPER

The *Dag Hammarskjold* takes off from Woomera, Australia for the new human settlement on Mars.

Planet Earth is being eaten away by uncontrollable pollution, starvation and disease. Its life expectancy is nil.

This is the last spaceship, its passengers the last people on earth with any hope. But it is never to reach its objective. Five thousand years later its captain wakes up to a new world undiscovered in his time and to a bitter experience he must fight alone.

CORONET BOOKS

SCIENCE FICTION FROM CORONET BOOKS

POUL ANDERSON

☐	16337 2	Beyond The Beyond	35p
☐	16336 4	Tau Zero	35p
☐	16480 8	Enemy Stars	35p
☐	16338 0	Rebel Worlds	35p
☐	18615 1	The Byworlder	35p
☐	19864 8	Ensign Flandry	65p

EDMUND COOPER

☐	10904 1	Five to Twelve	35p
☐	15132 3	The Uncertain Midnight	40p
☐	15091 2	The Last Continent	40p
☐	16464 6	Transit	30p
☐	19478 2	The Cloud Walker	35p
☐	16216 1	Kronk	35p
☐	20512 1	The Tenth Planet	60p

All these books are available at your local bookshop or newsagent, or can be ordered direct from the publisher. Just tick the titles you want and fill in the form below.

Prices and availability subject to change without notice.

～～～～～～～～～～～～～～～～～～～～～～～～～～～

CORONET BOOKS, P.O. Box 11, Falmouth, Cornwall.
Please send cheque or postal order, and allow the following for postage and packing:

U.K. – One book 18p plus 8p per copy for each additional book ordered, up to a maximum of 66p.

B.F.P.O. and EIRE – 18p for the first book plus 8p per copy for the next 6 books, thereafter 3p per book.

OTHER OVERSEAS CUSTOMERS – 20p for the first book and 10p per copy for each additional book.

Name ....

Address ....

....